TOGETHER for NEVER

TOGETHER FOR NEVER

By Marilyn Kaye

Printed and bound in January 2023 at Maple Press, York, PA, USA.
www.holidayhouse.com
First Edition
1 3 5 7 9 10 8 6 4 2

Library of Congress Cataloging-in-Publication Data is available.

ISBN: 978-0-8234-4612-4 (hardcover)

~ *To Sheila, Bertrand, and Diego.* ~

chapter one

The bell was still ringing in Charlotte's ears as she and her friends made their way toward the school exit. They were surrounded by jubilant classmates, shrieking and cheering. Cries of "Have a great summer!" filled the air.

Eighth graders Charlotte, Kendra, and Ashley were too cool to show excitement publicly like that, but once they were out the door, Ashley declared, "We're free!"

Kendra nodded fervently. "The last day of school. This has to be the best feeling in the world."

They both looked back at the building, glaring at it like it was a prison from which they'd all just been released. Charlotte looked back too, but she didn't see a prison. She was leaving a little palace where she'd reigned as queen for nine months. She had no doubt that she'd regain her position in September. But even so, it wasn't easy to leave behind.

In keeping with tradition, she initiated their usual walking-through-the-parking-lot game. They called it "Makeover." She indicated a girl just ahead of them.

"Lucy Kerr."

"Haircut," Kendra said. "Maybe one of those Brazilian straightening treatments. Those curls are out of control."

Charlotte nodded. There were some natural waves in her own shoulder-length blonde hair, but she tamed them every morning with an electric straightener comb.

"Mascara," Ashley suggested. "She has absolutely no eyelashes." She looked around for another worthy target. "Brittany Mills."

"Better shoes," Charlotte said promptly. "Those Mary Janes are disgusting. No one over the age of five wears those."

"And she needs a manicure," Kendra added. "Have you ever looked at her hands? She bites her nails, they're positively disgusting. Now, how about . . . Lily Holden?"

"Oh puh-leeze," Charlotte groaned. "I wouldn't know where to begin. She's utterly hopeless. I mean, *look* at her!"

They turned to stare at the small, slight girl with one long, dark braid hanging over her shoulder. Her gauze skirt was losing its hem, and half the stitches were missing from the embroidered blouse. In their American History textbook, there was a photo of hippies in the 1960s at a demonstration. Charlotte thought Lily Holden would have fit right in.

As usual, the girl was walking alone. She had to know that they were all looking at her, but her eyes were glued to the phone in her hand. With her other hand, she was tapping on the screen.

"Who could she be texting?" Ashley wondered. "She doesn't have any friends."

Charlotte nodded. "Even the other nerds think she's too weird. When are you going to camp?"

The conversation turned to summer plans—Ashley's tennis camp, Kendra's grandparents in the country house with a pool and horses.

"Is your father taking the cottage at Dipity?" Kendra asked Charlotte.

That was what everyone called Serendipity Bay, the beach town just under three hours away. Charlotte nodded. "We're going next week."

"What about your mother?"

"*Kendra*," Ashley murmured.

But Charlotte just gave a nonchalant shrug. "I'm not sure. I might visit her."

"Where is she now?" Ashley wanted to know.

Charlotte didn't have the slightest idea. "Paris," she guessed. It was possible. She knew Dahlia was in Europe, at least.

"Wow!" Kendra exclaimed. "You're going to Paris?"

"Or maybe Rome."

"So you'll meet the boyfriend?"

"*Kendra*!" Ashley hissed.

This was getting tiresome. Charlotte performed another shrug. "Mm . . . hey, what are you guys wearing tonight?"

This led into a discussion of the annual end-of-the-school-year party given by a friend, which lasted till they reached the corner where they separated to go to their respective homes.

For Charlotte, separating was a relief, in a way. Even though Kendra and Ashley were pretty much her best friends. But talking about her mother, carefully choosing the right words, not showing her feelings—it could be exhausting. And it wasn't like she was going to spill her guts, not even with her besties.

It was all pretty awful, though. Not to mention embarrassing. She'd heard of fathers leaving homes. But mothers?

Still, it wasn't as much of a shock as it would have been for most girls, Charlotte thought.

Dahlia Nettles had behaved strangely before. Many times, as a matter of fact. When Charlotte was only seven years old, her mother had taken off for India, to hang out with some guru and meditate for three months. And just two years ago, she'd decided she'd missed her chance to be a real actress. She regaled Charlotte with tales of how she'd been "*this close!*" to being in a movie before she met John Nettles and married him. So she'd gone to California, to see if she still had a chance of becoming a movie star. Apparently, she didn't, because she came back.

But she'd never been away *this* long before—eight months. And Charlotte's poor father had finally given up on her. Just a couple of months ago, he'd told Charlotte they were divorcing. Her mother had met a guy, twenty years younger than she was. He was a guitar player in some rock band Charlotte had never even heard of. And she was following him on the band's tour of Europe. Every now and then, Charlotte got an email from Dahlia—mostly about how well the band was doing and how happy she was. She always added that she missed Charlotte. Charlotte doubted this very much.

Aunt Molly, her father's sister, came to the rescue, just like she'd done in the past. She worked from her home, she didn't have a husband or kids, so she was available to help out, especially when Charlotte's father was off on one of his many business trips.

"What kind of mother would do something like this?" her aunt Molly had fumed.

My kind of mother, Charlotte replied silently.

It was funny, in a way. Growing up, Charlotte's friends all thought Dahlia was very cool. She was better looking and better dressed than their mothers. She never fussed about what Charlotte was wearing, and she let Charlotte wear eyeliner and mascara when the other girls could only use lip gloss. And Charlotte's friends actually talked to her, more than they talked to their own mothers. Because Dahlia didn't treat them like kids. They could tell her their problems, about their crushes on boys, stuff like that. And she told them stories about her wild and crazy life before she married, how she smoked weed and had affairs with celebrities.

Charlotte was never really convinced that all the stories were true, and sometimes she could be embarrassed by them, but that didn't really matter. Dahlia was *fun*. Not very motherly, maybe. Ashley used to say she was more like everyone's big sister.

And Charlotte missed her. She took comfort in one thing she knew for sure about her mother—nothing was forever. Dahlia would go full speed ahead with some new interest or project—yoga, art, dance lessons—but nothing lasted too long. She could get tired of this young boyfriend, she could lose interest in this band. She'd think about Charlotte. Maybe she'd think about her husband too.

Okay, they were officially divorced now. But Charlotte had heard of divorced couples getting back together.

Dahlia Nettles could still come home.

chapter two

Curled up on the sofa, Lily was on the last chapter of the latest Rulers of the Galaxy book. Normally a fast reader, she was trying to read slowly, to savor every word. It would be at least another year before the next book would appear, and she was trying to make this one last as long as possible. There was still the TV series, but next week's episode would be the finale of the season, and there'd be a long wait before the show returned.

Halfway through the chapter, she decided to save the last bit for reading in bed that night. She lay her bookmark on the page—Lily *never* bent page corners—and closed the book.

She gazed at the cover, with its magnificent portrayal of the characters who were currently struggling to take over the massive kingdom. What an incredible series. She hoped J. B. Calloway would never stop writing these books. He—or she—was the greatest writer ever.

Funny how nobody knew if J. B. Calloway was a man or a woman, or maybe nonbinary. He/she/they had a Facebook fan page, but there were no photos of the author, no pronouns were used—there was no personal information at all, just pictures of characters and book covers. Lily's #Galaxy followers on Twitter were constantly speculating on the sex of the author, trying to find clues in the books.

She wished she could write the author, just to tell him or her or they how much she loved the books. And tell him or her or they how she hoped to become a writer herself.

Maybe. She really didn't know. She loved to read, but she'd never tried to write anything, other than stuff for school.

She envied people who always knew what they wanted to be. Like Claire Miller, who ate lunch with her in the cafeteria. Claire had been taking ballet lessons since she was five, and she would be spending this summer at some famous ballet school in New York City.

Or like Suzy Phipps, her other lunchtime companion. She played the violin, and people already called her a prodigy. She was spending the summer away too, at a music camp.

So she wouldn't be seeing either of them again until

September. Not that she saw much of them anyway, except at lunch and in some classes. She didn't even know them that well. Claire's life was ballet, Suzy's life was violin. They spent all their time practicing or taking lessons, and neither of them read Rulers of the Galaxy or watched the show on TV. About the only thing they had in common was the fact that other kids thought they were all nerds.

Which was okay with Lily, if being a nerd meant that she wasn't like most of the other girls at school, giggling and gossiping, talking about boys, making endless trips to the Mall and wearing the same boring clothes from the same boring stores.

"Oh, come on," her mother would remonstrate when Lily spoke about her classmates. "They can't all be that bad."

But her mother smiled when she said this, and always ended up admitting she'd been a loner like Lily when she was thirteen, that she'd also wanted to be different from everyone else. Which made Lily feel good, since her mother was pretty much the most interesting person in the world. Well, next to J. B. Calloway. Lily wouldn't mind at all being just like her mother. Or J. B. Calloway.

Although, maybe the only interesting thing about J. B. Calloway was the fact that he/she/they wrote great books. Kate Holden was interesting in many ways. She could play the guitar and sing folk songs. She knew the names of birds.

She made great vegetarian meals. And she was a brilliant photographer.

That was one big difference between Kate Holden and Lily Holden. When her mother was thirteen, she knew what she wanted to be.

"I went to a photography exhibit at a museum. And the moment I saw what some people could do with a camera, I knew I would become a photographer."

And she did! The only problem was that she couldn't spend her days taking the kind of pictures she'd like to take—strange, thoughtful, unusual ones. She had to make a living for herself and Lily. So she took pictures at weddings and other celebrations. She was good at this, and people were always happy with her photos. But it was only in her free time that she could take the kinds of pictures she wanted to take.

Lily didn't think she wanted to be a photographer. Her mother had taught her how to use a camera, and sometimes they went out together to take pictures. But Lily just didn't get the kick out of it that her mother got. So maybe she should model herself after the one other person she considered interesting—J. B. Calloway. Which meant she really had to start writing.

But first, she'd check her tweets to see if anyone had anything interesting to say about Rulers of the Galaxy—the books or the TV series. She took her phone out of her backpack and started tapping.

Something was wrong. She wasn't connecting to the internet. Did she need to recharge it? No, the little battery picture was practically full. Suddenly, some odd wavy lines appeared on the screen. And then it went completely dark.

She stared at it in dismay. Frantically, she pressed more buttons, turning it on and off. She plugged it into a socket. Still, nothing happened.

"Lily, I'm home!"

Her mother's voice rang out from the hallway. Lily went out to greet her.

"What's wrong?" her mother asked immediately. That was another amazing thing about Kate Holden. She could practically read Lily's mind.

"My phone's broken."

"Oh dear. Sweetie, I hate to say I told you so, but—"

"I know," Lily said. She'd found the phone on a Chinese website. It claimed to have all the features of an expensive phone but for only ten dollars. Her mother had tried to talk her out of it, and offered to get her one of those pay-as-you-go phones, which were just for making calls. But Lily wanted to be able to tweet her Galaxy people when she wasn't home to use the family PC. So she'd spent her allowance on this piece of junk. And she'd gotten only two weeks of use out of it.

"How was work?" Lily asked as her mother followed her back into the living room.

Kate made a face. "Portrait photos for a business website. How was the last day of school?"

"Same as the first day," Lily replied. "But I think I've made a decision about what I'm going to do this summer."

Her mother set her camera bag down on the table. "And?"

"I'm going to write a novel."

Kate smiled widely. "Sounds like an excellent idea! You've got a great imagination, and I'm guessing that's a very important quality for a writer." She paused for a moment. "How would you like to write your book on the beach?"

"On the beach?" Lily's eyebrows shot up. "We're going to the beach?"

"John has rented a cottage there and invited us to stay."

"Who's John?"

Her mother rolled her eyes. "Lily, you've met him three times. *John,* John Nettles."

"Oh right, the suit."

Now Kate looked pained. "Lily, that's not nice. Yes, he wears a suit. He's a businessman. But he's also a very nice person. You said so yourself."

Lily drummed up a vision of the man her mother had been dating. Tall, grayish hair, a wide smile...

Yes, he'd been nice. So had been most of the men Kate dated. Her mother would never go out with a creepy guy. But the others had been a little less ordinary. She had particularly fond memories of a man with a bun who wrote poetry.

"Okay, that's cool. Sure, I could write on the beach." Sun, sand, waves... maybe it would inspire her!

"And his daughter will be with us too."

"He's got a daughter?"

Now her mother looked truly exasperated. "Lily, I told you that, ages ago! She's just about your age. In fact, she's probably at your school."

"Really?" And then, like a bolt of lightning had just hit her, she froze. "What did you say his last name is?"

"Nettles."

"And his daughter's name is...?"

Her mother paused to think. "Carla? No, that's not right. I only met her once..."

"Charlotte?"

"Yes, that's it! Do you know her?"

Lily wasn't frozen anymore. Now she was nauseous.

She said nothing. She and her mother made a quinoa salad for dinner. Then they watched an old movie on TV. At one point, Kate asked her why she was so quiet, and Lily told her she was thinking about the novel she was going to write. Her mother accepted that. And when she told her mother she was tired and going to bed, she accepted that too.

Lying in bed, Lily couldn't even open her book. Nothing, not even Rulers of the Galaxy, could distract her from her mother's news.

Charlotte Nettles. Of all the horrible girls at school,

the most horrible. The queen of the meanies. Just that day, walking through the parking lot at school, Charlotte and her obnoxious friends had been looking at her. And she knew they'd been saying something nasty, she could see it on their faces.

So this was going to be her summer. Sun, sand, waves.

And Charlotte Nettles.

chapter three

"I can't believe," Charlotte began, and then raised her voice to make sure her father would grasp the importance of what she was about to say. "I simply cannot believe you'd invite two complete strangers to come on vacation with us."

She wished he would turn to her so he could see the extremely distressed expression on her face. But he was driving, and his eyes were on the road. At least he had the courtesy to look a little concerned.

"They're not strangers, honey. I've been seeing Kate for three months and you've met her, remember? At the park? She was taking pictures."

Charlotte had a vague memory of a Sunday walk with her father and some woman with a camera around her neck. It just happened to be a day when her friend Kendra was having a crisis. After a polite "Pleased to meet you," Charlotte had been preoccupied, responding to Kendra's texts.

"And Lily's not a stranger either," her father continued. "You must know her at school."

"Yeah, okay, she's not a stranger. Just very, *very* strange."

Her father laughed, which was actually more annoying than if he'd scolded her.

"Oh, come on, honey," he said. "I've met Lily. She didn't seem strange to me."

Charlotte rolled her eyes. Like her father would have any idea what made a thirteen-year-old girl strange.

At least she wasn't having to spend nearly three hours in this car with the weirdo and her mother. Her father had told her that Kate had a job today, and she'd be coming later with Lily on the train.

When they paused at a stop sign, her father turned to her. He now wore that uneasy expression, which meant he was about to bring up something that made him uncomfortable to talk about.

"Does it bother you, Charlotte? That I'm seeing someone?"

"No," Charlotte replied promptly, and that was the truth. She knew he'd been going out with women, and she really didn't mind at all. After all, her mother was with another man, and her father deserved to have a social life.

The fact that he'd invited *this* woman on their vacation, though . . . Did that mean she was special?

Charlotte shivered.

"Cold?" her father asked. He turned off the air-conditioning and hit the buttons that opened the windows. Immediately, Charlotte smelled the salt air and her spirits lifted. For a few blissful moments, she forgot about Lily and her mother. And just as she'd done every year since she got her first cell phone, she whipped hers out and took a picture of the Welcome to Serendipity Bay sign by the road.

They'd been coming here since she was—well, for as long as she could remember. Sometimes, she wondered what it would be like to go somewhere more exciting—Disney World, maybe, or a glamorous exotic resort. But if she was going to be perfectly honest with herself, she had to admit that Dipity suited her just fine.

They were coming into the village now, the cute Main Street with its shops selling beach mats and big umbrellas, the stalls where artists and jewelry makers displayed their wares. Her father stopped in front of the post office.

"I'm just going to run in and pick up the keys."

"Do we need to get some groceries and stuff?" Charlotte asked.

"No, I called Miss Betty, and she's stocked the cottage for us."

Miss Betty ran the little café on the beach where you could get sandwiches and sodas and paper cups filled with the most delicious fried clams. Just the thought of those clams made her mouth water.

Her father returned, tossed the keys in her lap, and they took off. She knew it was childish, but she couldn't hold back a squeal of joy when she caught her first glimpse of the sea. Minutes later, they pulled into the driveway by the familiar white cottage with blue shutters.

While her father collected the luggage, Charlotte ran ahead with the keys and unlocked the door. There was a slight musty smell, but she knew it would disappear as soon as she opened some windows, which she promptly did. Sticking her head out, she took a deep whiff of salty air, and then turned to look around the living room.

She noted with satisfaction that everything was just as she remembered—the wicker furniture with the fat yellow cushions, the old wooden rocking chair, the framed pictures of sailboats on the walls. Then she went to her bedroom, to make sure nothing had changed in there. Nope—there were the frilly blue curtains at the window, the white dresser, the vanity table, the twin beds with their blue and white floral spreads.

That was when it hit her. She let out a shriek and ran back into the living room. Her father dropped the baggage and looked at her in alarm.

"What's the matter, honey? A bug?"

"Daddy! Do I have to share my room?"

"Well... yes, of course. There are only two bedrooms, Charlotte."

"No way, no way!" she wailed. "I can't, I just can't!"

"Don't be silly, Charlotte, you've shared that room before."

"With friends! With Ashley, with Kendra! Not with some creepy nerdy weirdo!"

Her father shook his head wearily. "Well, I'm afraid there's nothing to be done about it."

"Can't we change to a bigger cottage?" she begged.

"Charlotte, these cottages rent out months in advance. Nothing else will be available. Honey, please be reasonable."

Ohmigod, the horror of it all! She was debating which would be more effective—to burst into tears or to beg and plead when her father spoke again.

"Oh, I almost forgot. I have something for you!" He picked up his briefcase, rummaged through it, and extracted a small box. "It's the new iPhone! It just hit the stores today." He dangled it in her face like a fisherman with a tantalizing worm.

Typical John Nettles, Charlotte thought sadly. Trying to make up for things with a gift. For one very brief second, she considered rejecting it, just to show how really upset she was.

But on the other hand, even though she could usually twist her father around her little finger, it didn't look like she was going to get her way this time. And a brand-new, top-of-the-line iPhone—well, she wasn't made of stone. She had to melt.

And then there was that worried, hopeful, anxious-to-please expression on her father's face . . .

She accepted the box and even gave him a hug. "Thanks, Dad." Then she sighed deeply. "I'll share the room." Like she actually had a choice.

The phone would have to be charged before she could start using it, so she took it into the bedroom and plugged it in.

Back in the living room, her father was already setting up his laptop on the table in the adjoining dining room. There would be no more discussion of sharing rooms or anything else in the foreseeable future.

"I'm going to the beach," she announced.

His attention was already focused on the screen, but he did respond. "Be back by four, okay? I'm picking Kate and Lily up at the train station, and it would be nice if you came along."

Charlotte made a *hmm* sound that indicated she'd heard him but didn't actually confirm whether or not she'd be back in time.

She hadn't yet unpacked, and didn't want to take the

time to do it now, so she stuck her old phone in her pocket, and left the cottage wearing what she'd had on for the drive—cutoffs, a simple white tee, and sandals. Two minutes later she was at the top of the steps that led from the road to the beach. She paused, gazed out at the scene below, and let good feelings sweep over her.

The first day of vacation—this was the best, even better than the last day of school. Sun, sea, sand... people reclining on lounge chairs under big colorful umbrellas, kids lugging buckets and spades, a couple of guys with surfboards running into the water to catch a wave.

There were actually three beaches in Serendipity Bay. There was this one, which everyone just called "the Bay." A fifteen-minute walk in one direction would take you to a fancy luxury hotel with its own private beach, set off by jetties. It even had a fancy French name, La Plage. In the opposite direction was Rocky Beach. As the name suggested, the sand was covered with rocks and pebbles. People fished there during the day, and at night, teens went there to sit on the large boulders and fool around. At least, that's what she'd heard—she'd never actually been to Rocky Beach at night.

She went down the steps, slipped off her sandals, and buried her feet in the warm sand. A few feet away, a couple of little kids were building a sandcastle, and a memory came to her. She saw herself and a friend, maybe Kendra, smoothing the mound of wet sand and trying to make a turret. Her mother would have been nearby, lying on a lounge chair, her body all shiny from tanning oil. Her father... Would he have been there? Not that often, and when he *was* on the beach, he was on his cell with his office.

That was a long time ago. She wouldn't be building sandcastles this summer.

The sand was getting almost too hot, so she went down to the water's edge and let the cold water lap at her feet. Walking along, she spotted three girls on a blanket, playing a card game. They looked like they were around nine or ten, and another memory rose up in her mind. Just a few years ago, she'd met a couple of sisters here and she'd joined them almost daily for a few games of Uno.

She wouldn't be playing cards this summer either. She was thirteen years old, this was her first summer as an official teen. There would be no sandcastles, no Uno marathons. But she wasn't yet quite sure what there *would* be.

She could see Chez Betty, back up on the beach near the stone wall, and she was thirsty. Her feet were cold enough now to deal with the hot sand, and she moved quickly in that direction.

She crossed the stone terrace with its dozen café tables and chairs. It wasn't crowded—it was past lunchtime, and there were only a few people at the tables. She spotted Miss Betty herself at the counter and went there to greet her.

The woman smiled at her. "There you are, Charlotte! How are you? Everything okay at the cottage?"

"Perfect," Charlotte assured her.

"And your parents? How are they?"

"Well, it's just me and Dad this summer. Mom is... away."

"Ah." Miss Betty didn't ask any questions, but Charlotte thought she detected a little sympathy on her face. "Now, what can I get you?"

"Just a Coke, please," Charlotte said, and then she drew in her breath. "Oh no, I didn't bring my bag."

"No problem, my dear, you can owe me. And how about some fried clams to go with that?"

She wasn't really hungry—they'd stopped on the road for sandwiches. But just the thought of those fried clams made her suddenly famished. And she'd passed on the French fries at lunch...

"Yes, please."

Miss Betty beamed, as if she was thrilled by Charlotte's acceptance of the offer. Charlotte accepted the soda and the paper cup filled to the brim, thanked Miss Betty, and assured her that she—or more likely, her father—would pay her later.

She started toward one of the little tables when a chorus of laughter distracted her. A group—three guys, two girls—had just sat down at a larger table.

College kids, Charlotte thought. Sometimes a bunch of

them would rent a cottage together. But then she noticed the words on one boy's T-shirt: Riverside High School. Then one of the girls took off her huge sunglasses, and Charlotte could see how young she was. One of the boys said something she couldn't hear, but it made one girl shriek and the other start giggling.

So they were high school kids. Which meant they couldn't be more than four years older than she was, and maybe as few as two. She stepped behind a palm tree, where she could watch them without being seen stuffing her face with crispy clams.

They were a pretty good-looking group. A white boy with a deep tan looked particularly hot—tall, sun-streaked hair, nice strong-looking arms. The other two weren't half bad either. A deep-brown Black guy wasn't wearing a shirt and she could see that he actually had a six-pack. The other white boy was cute, lighter skinned, with a sprinkling of freckles on his face. He had shiny straight brown hair that fell into his eyes.

She assessed the girls. Both were pretty and had nice hair. The one who looked Asian had a very short cut with gelled spikes; the other, a tanned white girl, had long hair with pink streaks. Both flaunted good figures in their bikinis. The yellow bikini on one of them was exactly the same as the one in pale blue now sitting in her own suitcase.

Charlotte's figure was just as good as theirs—maybe even better, considering how flat-chested Pink Streaks was.

The longer she watched them, the more convinced she became that they weren't that old. Seventeen, tops, but probably more like fifteen. The boys were acting goofy, the girls were giggling.

All Charlotte needed was her own bikini, a little eyeliner and mascara, her hair up in a high ponytail, and she could pass as one of them. Yes, definitely.

She smiled. Now she knew what she'd be doing this summer. She slipped away, without even saying good-bye to Miss Betty, because that would mean those kids might see her in these baggy cutoff jeans that were so last year. Not to mention her childishly clean face.

She'd just arrived back at the cottage when the door opened and her father emerged, dangling the car keys from his hand.

"There you are! Coming to the station with me?"

Charlotte thought rapidly. "Oh, Dad, I just looked at my phone and saw an email from Mom. I was about to read it and the battery went dead."

He immediately went all sympathetic, just like she knew he would. "The Wi-Fi's working inside, honey, you can read it on your laptop. I'll be back in twenty minutes with our guests."

She supposed she should say something like "Yay" or "Can't wait," but she couldn't fake that much enthusiasm. But she managed a thin smile and an "Okay" before heading indoors.

That bit about her mother—it was a lie, of course. She hadn't even looked at her phone. But it was just a little white lie, and maybe not even that. For all she knew, there really *could* be an email from Dahlia waiting for her. She hadn't had one for a while.

But first, she had to set up the bedroom to make sure creepy Lily would know who the real occupant was. Opening her suitcase, she took out her Bluetooth speaker and set it up on the little vanity table that stood between the beds. Then she extracted the framed photo of herself with her parents and put that alongside the speaker. Finally, she opened her makeup case and emptied it on the remaining space. There would be no room for Lily's stuff—which didn't matter, because girls like Lily didn't wear makeup.

There were four drawers in the dresser. She divided her clothes between three of them, leaving only the bottom one empty. Lily would have to get down on her hands and knees to put her clothes away.

She sat on her bed and opened her laptop. Then she checked her email. It turned out that she hadn't lied at all—there it was, a message from Dahlia. She clicked on it.

It didn't take her long to read the whole thing.

Hey girl, what's happening? We're totally cool here in Spain. Jay and the boys got three encores in Valencia last night! It's crazy hot here, but at least I've got an amazing tan. We hit Madrid today, then back home tomorrow. Espadrilles are really cheap here, I bought myself three pairs today. I'll buy some for you too. What size? Miss you!

Charlotte sighed. Wouldn't a normal mother know her own daughter's shoe size?

Jay—that was the boyfriend's name. "The boys" were the other members of Molten Lava. Which, in her opinion, was a dumb name for a band.

She'd never met Jay, but she'd googled the band and saw him in a photo. He was okay-looking if you liked the type—personally, she always thought white guys with dreads looked kind of silly. Google also brought up an amateur YouTube video that showed the band performing. She didn't think much of the music.

She hit Reply and started typing.

Hi Mom, we're in Serendipity Bay. Everything's fine.

What else could she write? Should she tell her about the people who were coming? Knowing that her husband—ex-husband—was seeing someone might make her jealous. And that could be a good thing. Learning that another girl liked a guy always made the guy seem more desirable.

On the other hand, it just might signify to Dahlia that the marriage was really truly over. Charlotte reminded herself that legally, it really truly *was* over. But that didn't mean it couldn't start up again...

Thanks for the espadrilles. Size 6 1/2. Love, Charlotte

It wasn't much of an email but there wasn't much to write. Not yet, at least. She hit Send and closed her laptop.

chapter four

There wasn't much to see out of the window in the train—just buildings and fields, and no sign of the ocean yet. Lily turned to her mother sitting next to her, but Kate's eyes were closed. So she went back to the book she was reading. *Trying* to read.

In Another World was something new she'd picked up at the library. The cover declared that it was perfect for fans of Rulers of the Galaxy. Lily had only read one chapter, but already she completely disagreed. This book wasn't anywhere near as good. It was just an imitation.

Since she didn't have a phone anymore, she couldn't check any of her forums or Twitter to see what other Galaxy fans thought of it. The cloud that had settled on her head ten days ago darkened. Two weeks with no Galaxy chat.

She knew for sure that Charlotte wouldn't be interested

in talking about it. Girls like her, they probably didn't even read books at all, unless they had to, for school. As for TV shows, she knew from overhearing conversations that all they watched were those stupid teen shows about rich girls and their glamorous lives.

That was probably where they got their ideas about how to torment people who weren't in their crowd. Like the girl who posted a photo on Instagram of Alexis Gorham changing her clothes in the locker room after gym at school. It was taken behind Alexis, but you could tell from her bare back that she didn't wear a bra, and the girl taking the picture must have thought that was pretty funny. Maybe Charlotte herself didn't post the photo, but she probably clicked one of those heart icons to show she liked it.

What boggled Lily's mind was how other girls actually looked up to Charlotte and her crew. Even Lily's own lunch mate, Suzy, was absolutely thrilled once when Kendra Drake complimented her on a haircut. (Lily suspected that Kendra was being sarcastic, but Suzy didn't pick up on that.) As for Lily herself—more than once, she'd passed the popular girls' table in the cafeteria and didn't miss the way they'd glanced at her before putting their heads together and giggling hysterically.

Not that this really bothered her. She knew what they thought of her, and she was proud of it. She, Lily Holden, might be a weirdo—but Charlotte and her friends were scum. It made her wonder what kind of parents could create people like her. She'd never met Charlotte's mother, but John Nettles couldn't have been a very good father if he'd helped raise Charlotte.

Of course, Lily couldn't really know much about fathers, since she didn't have one. Naturally, there had to have been a biological father, but she'd never known him. According to her mother, *she'd* barely known him either. It had been a brief encounter, so brief that Kate Holden didn't even know his name.

It was too bad—she would like to have had a father, someone nice and caring, and then she wouldn't have to worry about who her mother was dating. Sometimes she had fantasies about who her father might be, what he was like, but most of what she conjured up in her head were just entertaining daydreams. There was no way her father could be Darius, the youngest son of Bartol, current ruler of the Galaxy kingdom...

But when it came to mothers, she'd totally lucked out in that regard. Kate wasn't just a mother, she was Lily's best friend. Even though she called her "Mom" to her face, in her mind she often thought of her as her pal, Kate.

She supposed she was okay with Kate going out with men—her mother deserved to have some fun. And she truly hoped her mother would find Mister Right. After all, Lily would leave home someday, and she wouldn't want Kate to be lonely. So far, though, there hadn't been anyone really special. There was that dentist, Doctor Something—he'd been nice, but kind of boring. And there was Alex the poet. He'd seemed pretty cool, but then he started borrowing money from Kate and not paying it back.

Beside her, Kate stirred, opened her eyes, and smiled. "Are we there yet?"

Lily grinned. "Hey, I'm the kid. I'm the one who's supposed to be asking that."

Her mother stretched. "I'm feeling like a kid today. Two weeks at the beach! I can't remember the last time I took a real vacation."

Lily looked pointedly at the camera that hung from Kate's neck. Kate caught the meaning.

"This is for fun, Lily. I won't be shooting a wedding or a birthday or a bar mitzvah. I'll be taking pictures of you and me, frolicking in the waves."

"And John," Lily added.

Kate cocked her head thoughtfully. "I'm not sure if John is a frolicking-in-the-waves type. But maybe we can talk him into it."

"You really like him, don't you?"

"I do," her mother replied promptly. "He's smart, he's kind, he's interested in so many things. We have great conversations."

"About what?"

"Oh, anything and everything! Books we've read, movies we've seen. Politics, current events."

"Do you agree on everything?"

"Not at all!" Kate laughed. "We had a major debate the other day about pizzas. Thin crust versus deep dish." Then her expression changed, and she made serious eye contact.

"Lily...I hope you get to know John better over the next couple of weeks."

Lily didn't avoid her eyes. "Why? Because this is serious?"

"I don't know yet," her mother replied. "I do know that I'm feeling very happy about our relationship. But Lily, you know that if it starts looking really serious, then you and I will talk about it. And if for any reason you're not comfortable..." Her voice trailed off, but Lily knew what she was saying. And it was a relief to hear.

"If you like him, I'll probably like him," she assured her mother. "I'm just thinking about Charlotte."

"But you don't really know her, do you? Give her a chance, sweetie. There may be more to her than you think."

Lily made a face, but her mother ignored that and went on. "You know, when I first met John, I didn't think he'd be my type at all. He seemed like such a straight businessman. I had to look beneath the suit..."

"Mom!"

They both started laughing. And they were still laughing as the train pulled into the station.

John Nettles was waiting for them on the platform. And now, he didn't look like a businessman at all. He was wearing sunglasses, khaki trousers with a faded green tee, and he wasn't carrying a briefcase. With a broad smile, he waved to them as they stepped off the train. On the platform, he kissed Kate on the cheek. Lily stepped back apprehensively, but he was totally cool—he didn't try to kiss her, but shook her hand instead.

"It's good to see you again, Lily."

She liked that—it sounded very adult. She nodded politely. "Nice to see you too, Mr. Nettles. Thank you for inviting me."

"Please, call me John! The car's right over there." Despite Kate's protests, he took both their suitcases. Lily had imagined the father of Charlotte Nettles would drive something big and fancy and shiny black, but it was just an ordinary blue car. He put the suitcases in the trunk, and Lily climbed into the back seat.

Just as she was adjusting her seatbelt, Mr. Nettles—John—turned to her.

"Oh, I've got something for you, Lily."

She wasn't shocked. The dentist used to bring little gifts for her all the time, and a couple of the other guys Kate went out with did too. She figured that was their way of sucking up to Kate and showing what nice guys they were.

But when she looked inside the bag he handed her, she *was* shocked.

"It's an iPhone!" she exclaimed.

"The latest model," John declared. "Just released this morning."

Her mother was shocked too, and she didn't look pleased. "John, we can't accept that!"

"Why not? You told me her phone broke."

"And I'll replace it," Kate said. "With something a lot cheaper than this. I know what iPhones cost."

John grinned. "Not for me. I have a friend in the electronics business. I give him free investment advice, he gives me free phones. I can get one for you too, Kate."

"No thanks, those things are way too complicated for me." She sighed. "Oh well, if it really didn't cost you anything... Lily, what do you say?"

Lily stared at the unopened box. "Um, thank you, Mr. Nettles."

"It's *John*!" He turned to face her and winked. "Call me 'Mr. Nettles' again and I'm taking it back!"

Lily opened the box and took a quick look at the instrument. It might be complicated, but she knew she'd be able to figure it out.

She couldn't help having mixed feelings about it, though. She supposed an iPhone would be very good for surfing and tweeting. But would that make up for the fact that she'd be carrying the same phone as those awful girls with their hundred-dollar haircuts and designer handbags? Girls like Charlotte Nettles?

She couldn't really start exploring it now. While she could read on a train, studying in a car always made her feel a little sick. So she looked out the window while her mother and John chatted up front.

She liked the look of the street they drove down. It was kind of old-fashioned, like a village, with some very cute little shops that didn't include those big chain stores and brand names that were at the Mall. When they came to an intersection, she caught glimpses of the sea, and her spirits rose.

And when John pulled into a driveway, she had another pleasant surprise. In the back of her mind, she'd imagined this summer house to be big and formal, a mansion, one of those places where you had to worry about knocking over a priceless vase. Instead, it was a sweet white cottage, with blue shutters, and flowers growing alongside the steps leading up to the little porch.

It was like a picture in a children's storybook, and even though it wasn't covered in gumdrops, for some reason she thought of Hansel and Gretel and the gingerbread house. But for all its cuteness, her spirits suddenly sank. Because she knew something about this gingerbread house that Hansel and Gretel didn't.

There was a witch inside.

chapter five

Sitting at the little vanity table, Charlotte looked into the mirror with one eye closed while she attempted to draw a precise line with black liquid eyeliner on the upper lid of the other. With the music blasting, she hadn't heard anything, but something made her look up.

That awful girl was standing in her doorway—small and skinny, with that one stupid braid, and wearing a T-shirt with Rulers of the Galaxy emblazoned on it. The sight made her lose her grip on the liquid pencil, and a black line suddenly extended practically to her ear.

Lily Holden's lips twitched, as if she was trying to hold back a laugh. Then she spoke, but Charlotte couldn't hear her. Reluctantly, she hit the pause button on her phone.

"What are you doing?" Lily asked.

Charlotte snatched up a tissue and rubbed at the mark on her face. "Practicing a cat's eye."

"A *what*?"

Fortunately, she didn't have to answer. Her father and the woman appeared behind Lily.

"Charlotte, you remember Kate Holden," her father said. "And you know Lily."

"Hello, Mrs. Holden." She didn't include Lily in the greeting. After all, they'd already spoken.

The woman smiled. "It's just Kate. Isn't this a pretty room, Lily?"

Lily nodded, but didn't say anything.

"How about something to drink?" John asked.

"I'd love a glass of water," Kate replied.

The adults disappeared. Charlotte wiped off the rest of the practice eyeliner, got up, and pointed. "That's your bed. And there's an empty drawer for your clothes."

"Okay."

Charlotte picked up her old phone and her handbag, left the room, and went out the back door.

They had a nice yard, surrounded by a white picket fence. A large palm tree provided some shade over the picnic bench. She sat down there, retrieved earbuds from her bag, put them on, and plugged them into her phone.

The music didn't do much to calm her nerves. It was strange, that she was feeling so tense. She'd been forewarned, she *knew* Lily Holden was coming, but the shock of actually seeing that creature, that total nerd, wearing that ridiculous T-shirt—no one over the age of ten wore T-shirts with TV shows on them.

And now here she was again, coming out the back door. With a brand-new, top-of-the-line, nobody-else-had-it iPhone in her geeky hands.

Charlotte leaped up and pulled out her earbuds. "What are you doing with my phone?" she demanded to know.

"It's *my* phone!" Lily declared.

John came out. His eyes darted back and forth between the two girls glaring at each other.

"Is something wrong?"

Lily spoke. "Charlotte thought this was her phone."

"Oh. Honey, I got one for Lily too."

Charlotte pressed her lips together tightly, to prevent herself from saying what she was thinking.

This was unbelievable. Absolutely, totally unbelievable. So her father hadn't given her the iPhone to make up for this intrusion on her summer. He'd given one to the intruder too. And what did this say about Charlotte being Daddy's special girl, his one and only adored daughter?

Lily's mother came out. "What a nice yard! Shall we cook out tonight?"

"I've got a better idea," John said. "It's our first evening here, and there hasn't been time for any serious grocery shopping yet. Let's go out to dinner. What do you think, Charlotte? The Barnacle Tavern?"

Blow after blow after blow. Every summer, on their first evening here, she and her parents went to the Barnacle Tavern for dinner. It was an annual family ritual. And now Dad wanted to bring this woman and her horrible daughter to join in on this tradition? This was just too awful. But what could she say, without infuriating her father?

"Now, how about a walk on the beach?" John suggested.

"Lovely," Kate said. "But about the restaurant—is it a fancy place? I didn't bring any dress-up clothes."

"No, no," John assured her. "It's totally casual, what you're wearing is fine."

Charlotte couldn't disagree with that. Kate's jeans were okay, and she wore a white ruffled top. A little too hippie for Charlotte's taste, but she had to admit it looked good on the woman.

Lily, on the other hand...

"Let me freshen up and I'll be ready for that walk," Kate said, and went back inside. John followed her.

As soon as they were alone outside, Charlotte spoke to Lily.

"You can't wear that to the Barnacle Tavern," she said, looking at the girl's T-shirt.

"Why not? Your father said it was casual."

There's casual, and there's pathetic, Charlotte thought,

but she couldn't be that rude. Not yet, at least. What if they ran into someone she knew at the Tavern? It had happened before. Just the thought of being seen with a companion wearing a Rulers of the Galaxy T-shirt . . . And those teenage kids from the beach could be there. Charlotte could *not* be seen with this girl.

Kate stuck her head out the door. "Ready for a walk on the beach, girls?"

"I'm not going," Charlotte said. "I've got stuff to do."

"Practicing your cat thing?" Lily asked.

Charlotte couldn't see a smirk on Lily's face, but she could *feel* it.

"Have you got a cat?" Kate asked.

"No," John said, and he turned his puzzled face to Charlotte.

"Just a joke," Charlotte said shortly. "Um, my clothes are really wrinkled, I want to iron something to wear tonight."

Now her father looked even more puzzled, since he'd never seen Charlotte iron anything in her life. Finally, the three of them left.

So Lily Holden can be nasty, Charlotte thought. She hadn't expected that.

Maybe it wasn't such a bad thing. Because Charlotte Nettles could be even nastier. And now she wouldn't even have to feel bad about it.

chapter six

She probably shouldn't have said that, about the cat's eye, Lily thought as she followed the adults down the road. On the other hand, why wait and let Charlotte be cruel first? She remembered an article she'd once read in one of her mother's magazines, about how women should be proactive instead of reactive. They probably weren't talking about who should make the first nasty crack.

So far, so bad. First, she discovered she'd be sharing a bedroom with snotty Charlotte. Then Charlotte accused her of stealing her phone. And now, here she was, tagging along after her mother and Mr. Nettles—John—and thinking that any minute they'd start holding hands. This was something she'd rather not see. Every few seconds Kate turned and looked at her anxiously. Lily knew she should smile, to let her mother think she was fine and perfectly happy, but she just couldn't drum up the energy.

She was only half listening as John described Serendipity Bay.

"...the hotel down that way is really luxurious, celebrities go there. And back the other way is Rocky Beach, not great for sunbathing or swimming but very pretty."

Lily realized a potential for escape. "I'd like to see that," she said quickly. "Mind if I go by myself? Then you guys can have some time alone."

Her mother looked at her with concern in her eyes. Lily presented a bright smile, probably her first smile since they arrived.

"I suppose that's alright," Kate said, looking at John.

"It's perfectly safe here," John assured her. "See that café over there? Chez Betty? Let's meet there in thirty minutes."

After she'd left them, Lily realized she wasn't wearing a watch and she'd left her new phone in the cottage. Oh well...if she wasn't there precisely on time, they probably wouldn't miss her.

Sand was getting into her sneakers, so she took them off. Then she moved down to the shoreline and let the water lap at her feet as she walked. It felt good, but not good enough to make her feel better all over.

This thing between her mother and John, this relationship... it seemed different from the relationships she'd had before, but she wasn't sure why. She hadn't been around them together, not really. But there was something about Kate's expression when she said his name. The way they looked at each other... or maybe she was just imagining this. True, he did seem nicer than any of those old boyfriends. But at least none of those old boyfriends came with a Charlotte.

In the heat, she shivered, as if she'd felt a chill. How was she going to get through this so-called vacation?

Lost in her thoughts, she suddenly realized that the sunbathing crowd on the beach had disappeared, and then she winced when her foot came down on a sharp pebble. The sand was gone, and she was now walking on stones. Just ahead was a large boulder, with a deep indentation that looked like it could be a place to sit. She hobbled over to it, pulled herself up into the ridge, and rubbed the sore spot on her foot. Then she looked around.

It was pretty here! She was practically alone on the beach. Along the jetty, there were three fishermen dangling lines into the water. They could have been statues, they were so still. Farther out in the sea, she spotted a few sailboats. Instead of suntan oil and fried foods, she could smell the salt water. Without the yelling and shouting of children, she could hear the soft crash of the white-crusted waves. And there was blue, beautiful blue, as far as her eyes could see.

All her tension seemed to melt away, and a new feeling came over her—not happiness, exactly, but peace. Now she could envision a real vacation. She would come here every morning and stay all day. Pack a sandwich, or buy one at that café, so she wouldn't even have to go back to the cottage for lunch. This was the perfect escape, from Charlotte, from whatever her mother and John were up to.

She could write her novel here! Along with the sandwich, she'd bring a notebook and a pen. She'd sit right here, on this boulder, with no one to bother her or look over her shoulder. The more she thought about this, the more excited she became. She could make this vacation tolerable—better than tolerable.

But now she had to make a decision. What kind of novel would she write? It would be about a girl, of course. Lily just didn't know enough about boys to write about them. And she knew what the girl's name would be: Sierra. She'd seen that name somewhere, and she'd thought it was beautiful.

Maybe it would be a mystery. Sierra walks along a beach and a body washes ashore. It's someone she knows. The police think the girl drowned, but Sierra knows the girl had a dangerous secret. Now Sierra has to find the killer.

Or it could be a fantasy. Sierra would be a mermaid,

leading all the other mermaids in a battle against evil lobsters for control of the sea. Sort of an underwater version of Rulers of the Galaxy.

Or Sierra is a lifeguard and she rescues a surfer when he falls off his board and starts to drown. He turns out to be someone very important, like a politician or a movie star, and Sierra becomes famous for saving him.

Well, she didn't have to decide right this minute. Maybe just staring out at the sea and daydreaming would bring the best idea out. She could see herself now, sitting out here all day, composing the story. Maybe she'd even come out in the evening with a flashlight.

She figured it was probably about time to meet her mother and John at that café. Reluctantly, she jumped down from the rock, cast one last longing look at the deep blue sea, and headed to the other beach. She'd timed it well—just as she approached Chez Betty, her mother and John arrived from the opposite direction.

In a much better mood now, Lily greeted them brightly. "Did you have a nice walk?"

Her mother nodded. "We went all the way to the other side, just by the private beach. There's an inlet with the loveliest nooks and crannies. Tomorrow I'm bringing my camera."

The gray-haired woman behind the café counter waved

to them, and John waved back. Lily and Kate followed him to the counter, where he kissed the woman on her cheek.

"Betty, thanks for taking care of the cottage. Let me introduce Kate, and her daughter Lily. They're staying here with us."

Betty greeted them warmly. "Funny, your daughter didn't mention any guests. I saw her earlier."

"Which means I must owe you some money," John said.

While the adults talked, Lily looked around the café. Here on the stone-paved terrace, there were about a dozen tables, four of which were occupied. One table in particular caught her attention. A bunch of teenagers were horsing around, tossing French fries at one another and trying to catch them in their mouths. It looked pretty disgusting. The girls were squealing and the boys were laughing like maniacs as the fries flew across the table. One of them knocked over his soda as he made a particularly vigorous effort to catch a fry. The glass fell to the ground and broke. A couple nearby looked annoyed, picked up their drinks, and moved to another table.

When one French fry landed on the plate of another customer, he got up and glared at them furiously. He took a step toward them.

Fortunately, the café lady—Betty—saw this and came out from behind the counter.

"Okay, kids, cut it out right this minute or you're banned for the summer."

They settled down, but the second Betty turned away, one of the boys made a nasty gesture toward her and the girls giggled.

What creeps, Lily thought, and as she headed back to the cottage with her mother and John, she made a mental note to bring a sandwich from home tomorrow, so she wouldn't have to come back here to the café.

When they entered the cottage, Charlotte came out of her bedroom. She'd changed her clothes, and Lily wasn't at all surprised by her new outfit—it was so typical of Charlotte's crowd. White jeans with rips that had been carefully placed, perfectly even at the knees. Lily had seen jeans like this in shop windows and magazine advertisements, and she couldn't understand why anyone would want to buy clothes that were torn. But she knew they were the fashion, so of course Charlotte would have them. On top, she had on a white tank that stopped at least four inches above the jean's waistband.

"Are we all ready to head out to the restaurant?" John asked her. "I'm just going to change my shirt."

"I want to wash my hands," Kate said.

As soon as they were gone, Charlotte turned to Lily.

"Don't you want to change *your* T-shirt?" she asked.

"No," Lily said. "Why should I?"

"It's embarrassing," Charlotte hissed.

"Not to me," Lily replied.

To be perfectly honest, she was feeling a little grungy, a little sweaty, and before Charlotte opened her big mouth, she'd actually been thinking about changing her shirt before they left.

But now she wouldn't give her the satisfaction.

chapter seven

The Barnacle Tavern wasn't the fanciest restaurant Charlotte knew, and she'd been to many restaurants. Her mother was never much into cooking. The Nettles family had gone out to eat frequently—sometimes the three of them, but since her father was out of town a lot, it had usually been just Dahlia and Charlotte. Dahlia loved to dress up and go to trendy places where she could drink wine with her meal. She'd always let Charlotte have a sip, and Charlotte always pretended to enjoy it.

But even though it wasn't trendy or fancy, the Barnacle Tavern was one of her favorite places, and she always ordered the same thing—fish and chips. As they were driving there, she tried not to think about the fact that this was the first time she'd be going to the Barnacle without her mother. Instead, she concentrated on the meal to come—that delicious light, crunchy, sweet fish and the crispiest French fries in the world.

She glanced at Lily, sitting next to her in the back seat. The girl wore that same tense expression that had been on her face all day. Maybe she was nervous about where they were going. Charlotte figured that Lily didn't have much experience with restaurants.

She had no interest in soothing any anxieties Lily might have about this, but she also didn't want Lily to do something embarrassing when they arrived.

"The Barnacle is not like McDonald's, you know. You don't order from a counter, there are waiters who come to the table."

Lily rolled her eyes. "For your information, I *have* been to restaurants where there are waiters. And I *never* go to McDonald's."

Charlotte's eyebrows went up. "You're kidding!"

"We don't eat meat."

The use of *we* instead of *I* indicated she was talking about her mother too. Now Charlotte could feel her eyebrows practically meeting her hairline.

"You're a vegetarian?" She looked toward the front of the car. Did her father know this? The man who loved nothing more than a big fat juicy steak—did he know that the woman sitting next to him was a vegetarian?

Kate turned around toward her with a smile. "Actually,

we're pescatarians. We don't eat red meat or poultry, but we do eat fish."

"Why?" Charlotte asked. Then she frowned. "Is it like some sort of religious thing? Are you in a cult?"

Kate laughed. "No, no, nothing like that."

Her father spoke. "Charlotte, Kate doesn't have to explain herself."

"It's alright," Kate said. "It's just a personal philosophy, Charlotte. It doesn't bother me if other people eat meat. I just don't feel comfortable with the way animals are raised to be slaughtered. And supposedly, fish aren't sentient."

"*Sentient* means having feelings," Lily said to Charlotte.

"I knew that," Charlotte snapped. Actually, she'd never heard the word before, but she wasn't about to give Lily any credit for the definition.

But how could they know that fish didn't have feelings? She didn't ask, because she didn't want to continue this conversation. They'd arrived, they were getting out of the car, and what if someone overheard them talking about fish feelings?

At least Kate and Lily would be able to eat here. The Barnacle Tavern was mainly a seafood restaurant. Just inside the door, there was a huge glass tank full of live lobsters crawling around. Lily seemed to be curious about this, and as they waited for someone to come and seat them, she moved closer to the tank.

"They're kind of crowded in there," she said.

"What do *you* care?" Charlotte asked. "You just said, they don't have feelings."

Lily shrugged. "Even so . . ."

"Well, don't worry about it," Charlotte said, and exaggerated the word *worry* so her sarcasm would be clear. "They won't be in there for long."

"Do they get put back in the ocean?"

Ohmigod, she was just too stupid. Charlotte lowered her voice so the adults wouldn't hear. "*No.* It's one of the specialties here. People choose the lobsters they want to eat. Then they're scooped out and cooked."

Lily's eyes went wide. "You mean, a customer decides which one is going to die?"

Charlotte was almost enjoying this. "And then the lobster is boiled. Alive."

Lily gasped. "Oh no! That's terrible!"

Her voice had risen, and caught the adults' attention. As Lily told them what she'd just learned about the poor lobsters, Charlotte edged away from the group and positioned herself in a spot where she could survey the dining room.

She didn't see anyone she knew at the tables, but there was a face she recognized. It was one of the boys she'd seen at Chez Betty—the blond one. He wasn't with the other teens this time. The people at his table were an older man and woman. His parents, she decided. And a younger boy.

The adults were talking to each other while the little boy seemed to be playing a game on a phone. The good-looking older boy was slumped back in his seat. He looked bored.

She heard her father say, "Table for four, please," and she turned to him.

"I'm going to wash my hands," she announced, heading off in the direction of the restrooms.

This little detour would serve two purposes, she thought happily. First, the boy wouldn't see her walking through the restaurant with a girl wearing a Rulers of the Galaxy T-shirt. Secondly, she now had time to check her makeup and fix her hair in preparation for—hopefully—him noticing her as she passed his table.

Minutes later, she left the ladies' room and sauntered casually through the dining room. When she passed the boy's table, she glanced in his direction. Luck was with her—he looked back. Eye contact!

Nothing was said, and they didn't even smile at each other, but the eye contact was enough. She'd be able to speak to him on the beach the next day—"Didn't I see you at the Barnacle Tavern last night?"—or maybe she could come up with something more clever.

By the time she arrived at the table where her father, Kate, and Lily were sitting, they were giving their orders to the waiter. The adults were seated side by side, which meant she had to sit next to Lily. Well, that was better than sitting across from her, and having to look at her while she was eating.

"And for you, young lady?" the waiter asked. "Would you like a moment to look at the menu?"

"That won't be necessary," her father said. "She knows what she wants, don't you, Charlotte? Fish and chips, please."

"Just like Lily!" Kate exclaimed. "She loves fish and chips too."

Okay, maybe she was being silly, but she just couldn't stand the idea of having anything in common with that girl.

"Actually, I think I'll try something new," Charlotte said quickly. She opened the menu and scanned it quickly. Mussels . . . she knew they were little shellfish things, and they might be like those fried clams at Chez Betty. And according to the menu, they came with French fries. So if she wasn't crazy about the mussels, she'd still have something to eat.

She gave her order and the waiter took their menus. After he left, there was a moment of silence at the table. Her father broke it.

"So . . . do you girls have any classes together?"

"No," Charlotte said.

"Yes we do," Lily corrected her. "Geometry."

"Oh. Sorry." She tried to come up with an excuse for herself. "I really have to concentrate in Geometry. I guess I never noticed who's in the class."

Lily rolled her eyes, which Charlotte ignored.

"What's your favorite class, Charlotte?" Kate asked.

"Um . . . I like History. Mr. Clark is cool."

Lily made a face. "Really? You think he's cool?" Turning to the adults, she said, "He tries to act like he's one of us, making stupid jokes and talking about how he loves rap music."

"Well, that's better than acting like a fussy old lady. Like Ms. Hanover. She's a real . . ." She reminded herself she wasn't with Dahlia and had to watch her language. "A really mean lady."

Lily was shaking her head vigorously. "I adore Ms. Hanover! She makes literature come alive. We've got a lot of idiots in my class, so it's not easy for her. Like, Ashley Carson. She gave a report on *The Book Thief*. It's historical fiction, about a girl in Germany during World War II. And Ashley said it was a fantasy!"

Charlotte looked at her coldly. "Ashley Carson is one of my best friends."

Lily shrugged. "That doesn't stop her from being an idiot."

"Lily!" Kate exclaimed. "That's not very nice!"

"Yeah, okay. Sorry."

Fortunately, the waiter arrived just then with their food. While the adults exclaimed over how good everything looked, Charlotte examined her bowl of mussels in disappointment. From the look of the things, these were definitely nothing like Miss Betty's clams. They weren't crispy at all. And you had to dig the things out of their shells yourself. When she managed to get one out with her fork, it looked like a giant version of something that could come out of your nose.

Her father was looking at Lily's T-shirt. "Is that the name of a rock band, Lily?"

"No, it's a TV show, and a book," Lily told him.

"What's it about?"

"It's about a mythical universe, where there are kingdoms on each planet, and characters battle for control of the whole galaxy. There are all these elaborate schemes, and the characters are really interesting."

Now it was Charlotte's turn to roll her eyes, and she made sure that Lily saw her expression.

"Do you watch this show, Charlotte?" her father asked.

"*No*," she replied, and it came out with even more force than she intended. "I don't like fantasy shows. I prefer more realistic ones."

"Like *The Very Best Girls*?" Lily asked.

"How did you know?" Charlotte asked.

"Just an educated guess."

Charlotte looked at her suspiciously. Was that another insult?

"What's *that* show about?" her father asked.

Charlotte shrugged. "It's just about some high school girls, that's all."

"I've heard of that one," Kate remarked. "It's always described as *aspirational*."

Charlotte's father looked curious, and she explained. "The girls are all beautiful, they wear expensive clothes, and they're very glamorous. They have the lives viewers can only daydream about."

John frowned. "That doesn't sound very... I don't know... appropriate? In terms of values, I mean."

Charlotte looked at him anxiously. She had never heard her father talk about "values" before. Was this Kate's influence? Was he going to suddenly forbid her from watching her favorite show?

But Kate came to her rescue. "Oh, I think it's just a fun thing for girls, some escapism from their ordinary lives. Isn't that right, Charlotte?"

"Exactly," Charlotte said. She had to admit, Kate was a lot sharper than her daughter. "It's fun, that's all. I mean, who wouldn't want to be beautiful and wear fabulous clothes?"

"It's not what *I* aspire to," Lily commented.

Charlotte couldn't resist. "No, you aspire to live on another planet, right?"

Lily glared at her. "Well, I'd rather be an alien than a spoiled brat."

"Well, I'd rather be spoiled than, than"—she mentally searched for a word that would suit Lily—"than pathetic!"

"Charlotte!" her father exclaimed, while at the same time, Kate cried, "Girls, please!"

There was a tense moment of silence and everyone looked uncomfortable. Then, practically in unison, both girls muttered "Sorry." Charlotte wasn't being sincere, of course. And Lily didn't sound like she meant it either.

Lily picked up her utensils and dug into her fish. Charlotte stuck the booger-thing into her mouth. It didn't taste bad, but it was a combination of chewy and slimy, and she had to force herself to swallow it. Well, at least she had fries.

She picked up the bottle of ketchup that sat on the table and held the spout over her French fries. Pounding the bottom, she finally managed to get a blob to fall out.

"May I have the ketchup, please?" Lily asked, without looking at Charlotte.

Charlotte didn't look at her either. With the bottle still upside down, she extended it toward Lily—a little too forcefully. Another blob fell out—right on Lily's T-shirt.

Lily gasped. Charlotte turned to see a large red stain spreading over the word *Galaxy*. All she could think to say was "Oops."

For a second, Lily seemed frozen, and Charlotte watched her uneasily. Was the girl going to burst into tears? She looked like she wanted to.

But with her lips pressed together tightly, Lily took her napkin and wiped off the ketchup. Kate signaled the waiter and asked for more napkins.

"Charlotte, don't you want to say something to Lily?" her father demanded to know.

"Uh, yeah, okay, I'm sorry. But it was an accident."

"You did that on purpose!" Lily declared hotly.

"Did not!"

Kate dipped another napkin in water and handed it over to her daughter. "Oh Lily, why would Charlotte do something like that on purpose? Because she doesn't watch your TV show? Don't be silly!"

"We have a washing machine at the cottage," John assured Lily.

"This will never come out," Lily said as she rubbed the stain with the napkin.

"Well, then, we'll get you a new one."

Lily shook her head. Her lips were so tightly clenched, Charlotte thought that it was amazing she could get any words out. "I bought it online, and it's not available anymore."

John looked at Kate helplessly.

"Lily, don't make such a fuss," her mother said. "It's just a T-shirt."

"It's the principle of the thing," Lily muttered.

Charlotte knew what Lily meant. She was saying that

Charlotte threw ketchup on the T-shirt because she didn't like it and she wanted to hurt Lily.

Which wasn't true, of course. Okay, the part about not liking the T-shirt was true. But she didn't *mean* for the ketchup to end up on it.

At least, she didn't *think* she did it on purpose. She'd read somewhere that sometimes your subconscious desires made you do things you didn't intend to do. Did she hate Lily's T-shirt enough to spill ketchup on it? Did her subconscious make her do it?

That meant she must have a pretty mean subconscious. But at least now she wouldn't have the embarrassment of being seen with Lily while she wore it over the next two weeks. Because, like Lily said, there was no way even a good hot wash would get all that red out.

And maybe she'd even done Lily a favor! People wouldn't be laughing at her.

There wasn't much more conversation during the rest of the meal. The parents occasionally said something about the food and the restaurant, while Lily silently shoved food in her mouth. Charlotte ate her French fries and thought about which of her three bikinis she'd wear on the beach tomorrow.

They didn't order dessert.

"Just before we left, I saw a carton of ice cream in the freezer," her father announced. "Miss Betty brought it with our groceries. Mint chocolate chip."

"Lily, that's your favorite," Kate said. Clearly, she was trying to cheer up her sulking daughter.

Lily just shrugged.

When they got back to the cottage, Charlotte checked on her new iPhone. It was completely charged now, so she sat on her bed and started downloading apps. Lily came in and changed her T-shirt. Charlotte politely didn't watch, but she couldn't resist a glimpse and a sigh of relief when Lily pulled the fresh T-shirt over her head. There was no writing on it.

"Ice cream, girls!" Kate called out.

Reluctantly, Charlotte dragged herself off the bed. Still clutching the phone, she went to the table.

"Do you want something to drink with that?" her father asked as he placed bowls of mint chocolate chip on the table. "There are juices and sodas in the fridge."

"Is there any Diet Coke?" Charlotte asked.

"Why do you want a diet drink?" Kate asked her. "You have a perfect figure!"

Charlotte tried to look modest. "Thank you."

Kate moved closer to her. "And you know, I've read that the sweet stuff they put in the diet drinks is even worse for you than real sugar."

"Really?" She had to admit, it was nice the way Kate was speaking to her, like an adult. The woman was really so much cooler than her daughter.

"How about you, Lily?" John called from the kitchen. "Come look and see if there's anything you'd like."

When Lily emerged from the kitchen, she was carrying a glass of juice in one hand and a Coke in the other. She handed the bottle to Charlotte.

"Do you want a glass for that?" she asked.

Charlotte was surprised at how gracious Lily was acting. She began to feel almost guilty about the ketchup.

"Um, no, I don't need a glass. Thanks."

She twisted off the cap, and immediately an enormous spray of soda flew out of the bottle. Stunned, Charlotte could only gasp. Her white T-shirt and her white jeans were soaking up the brown liquid.

"Oops," Lily said.

Charlotte leaped up and found her voice. "You shook it!" she screamed.

Her wail brought Kate and John out from the kitchen. In unison, they cried, "What happened?"

"Lily shook the Coke bottle so it would explode all over me!"

"It was an accident," Lily declared. "I didn't shake it."

"I don't believe you! You're trying to get back at me for the ketchup!"

"No I'm not!"

"Hey, you two, stop it right now!" her father demanded. "Accidents happen." He looked at Kate, and Charlotte could see the worry on his face. Despite her anger, she was almost glad. Maybe now he was starting to regret this whole vacationing-together thing.

Kate went back into the kitchen and came out with a roll of paper towels. She handed it to Charlotte, who began blotting the liquid.

"We'll just do a load of wash, first thing in the morning," Kate said calmly. "Now, come on everyone, let's just sit down and enjoy our ice cream."

At this point, Charlotte was so *not* in the mood for ice cream. Still, a dinner of French fries had left her hungry, so she picked up her spoon. But in the back of her mind, she was envisioning some possible way she could accidentally on purpose empty her bowl over Lily's head.

chapter eight

Helping herself to some cereal the next morning, Lily watched as her mother added Charlotte's white jeans and the Galaxy T-shirt to other stuff in the washing machine.

"That ketchup will never come out," Lily commented.

"Maybe, maybe not," Kate said. "But look, Lily. I know it's your favorite TV show and your favorite T-shirt, but it's just a TV show and it's just a T-shirt. It's not all that important and you know it. I don't understand why you're making such a fuss."

Lily didn't say anything. How could she possibly explain to her mother that this was more than a TV show and a T-shirt? It was *symbolic,* of what people like Charlotte thought they could get away with, of how they could treat other people. Like, if you weren't one of the elite, the cool ones, the popular kids, you were nothing. And Lily Holden was not nothing.

She took her cereal into the dining area, and she was just sitting down as John came out from the bedroom. He greeted Lily with a smile.

"Good morning!"

He really had a nice smile, very sincere, Lily thought. And once again she wondered how he could have such a nasty daughter. She echoed his words with a smile of her own.

Kate emerged from the kitchen and picked up her handbag. "I'm ready," she told John.

"Where are you guys going?" Lily asked.

"To the market," Kate said. "Want to come?"

Lily glanced through the window, where blue skies and sunshine seemed to be calling her name.

"No thanks, I'm going to the beach."

"Sounds like a plan," John said. "Where's my daughter?"

"Still sleeping," Lily said, silently adding *lazy dog.*

John looked at his watch and frowned. "Well, wake her up and you two can go to the beach together."

It took real effort not to roll her eyes again while he was looking at her, but she managed. She went back to the bedroom and stuck her head in.

"Charlotte, want to go to the beach?" she asked loudly.

The girl in the bed barely shifted, but she let out a noise that signified something negative.

Lily returned to the adults. "I don't think she wants to go right now. I guess we'll get together there later."

Her mother gave her a big smile of approval, and she and John left the cottage.

Lily went back to the bedroom, took her swimsuit and a big T-shirt from the drawer, and brought them into the bathroom. It wasn't modesty that kept her from changing in the bedroom. She just wasn't in the mood for Charlotte to wake up and comment on her very plain green tank-style suit. Or the oversize Hello Kitty T-shirt. She'd only planned to wear that T-shirt as a nightgown, but she had a feeling it would annoy Charlotte almost as much as the Galaxy tee. So she would wear it out, and embarrass her publicly.

She slipped her feet into her flip-flops, tossed a notebook, a pen, her wallet, her book, and the new iPhone in a shopping bag, and took off. Outside, it was even warmer than she thought it would be. And by the time she reached the steps leading down to the beach, she was hot.

So hot. Really, really hot. Once she hit the sand, she could almost feel the heat penetrating the soles of her flip-flops. The clear blue water before her with its foam-encrusted waves looked very inviting.

She was tempted to go in for a quick dip. But what would she do with her bag? Just leave it on the beach while she ran into the water?

It would probably be safe. Looking around, she saw

families with children, two women in bikinis stretched out on beach towels, an elderly couple sitting on plastic chairs under a big umbrella, two kids kicking a soccer ball back and forth . . . but then, not too far away, she spotted a group who looked familiar. She was pretty sure they were the obnoxious kids she'd seen at Chez Betty the day before. And she thought they were just the kind of people who would grab a bag and take whatever was inside.

Then a man approached, with a big basket hanging from one arm and carrying a beach umbrella and a folding chair under his other arm. Each of his hands clutched the hand of a small child. Just alongside Lily, he dropped the basket, took out a big beach blanket and a folding chair, and dumped the rest of the contents onto the blanket—plastic buckets, shovels, a beach ball. The children pounced on the stuff. The man then set up the umbrella, opened the folding chair, took a paperback book out of the basket, and flopped down into the chair with a big sigh.

"Excuse me," Lily said to him. "I want to run into the water for a couple of minutes. Could you keep an eye on my bag?"

"Sure," the man said. "I'll put it under my chair to protect it from wild animals." He nodded in the direction of the happily occupied children.

"Thanks," Lily said. She pulled off her T-shirt, stepped

out of her sandals, and ran as fast as she could, before the sand could burn her feet.

There was a brief moment of shock as the cold water hit her skin, but it subsided quickly, and then the water was gorgeous. She hopped around for a moment and considered swimming to the pier, but decided she'd rather float on her back and just stare up at the cloudless sky. So relaxing... she could actually feel all the tension in her head and her body just draining away. Even the image of Charlotte Nettles was fading...

Oof! A soccer ball fell on her stomach. It didn't hurt, but it stunned her and she curled up in the water. She flailed around for a few seconds until her feet found the floor.

"Sorry!" two young boys called out.

"It's okay," she called back, and tossed the ball in their direction.

She made her way back to the shore and the man with the two children. As she approached, he looked up from his book, then reached under the chair for her plastic bag.

"Thanks, I appreciate it," Lily said, taking the bag.

"Can I ask you to return the favor? Could you stay here for a couple of minutes and keep an eye on them? I forgot to bring a bottle of water, and if I take those two to the café with me, they'll start begging me for..." he lowered his voice and spelled out "i-c-e c-r-e-a-m."

"Sure, no problem," Lily said. Babysitting wasn't really her thing, but the two little girls seemed happily preoccupied with dumping buckets of sand on each other.

"Thanks, what's your name?" he asked.

"Lily."

"I'm Martin." He rose from his chair and spoke to the kids. "Rose, Sarah, this is Lily. She's going to stay with you for a few minutes. I'll be right back."

Looking at them more closely now, Lily realized the girls looked exactly alike. "Twins?" she asked.

Martin nodded. "Rose is the one with the freckle on her nose."

That one, Rose, looked up at him. "Can we go swimming?"

"No, you stay right here, you do *not* move from that spot. Thanks, Lily, I'll be as fast as I can."

Lily sat down on the blanket, and the other twin, Sarah, lifted her bucket of sand with the clear intention of dumping it on Lily's head.

"No!" Lily yelled.

Sarah's lower lip trembled, and Lily tried to think of something to say to ward off her howling.

"Hey, do you girls have any books here? I could read you a story."

Rose pointed to the straw basket.

"Okay, go get it."

"Daddy said we can't move."

Well, at least they were obedient. Still, Lily kept her eyes on them as she edged backward, stuck her hand into the basket, and felt around for the book.

Looking at the cover, she saw that it was a picture book of Cinderella. She held it up. "Is this okay?"

Two heads bobbed up and down, and Lily moved back onto the blanket. Personally, even as a small child, she hadn't really liked the story. She couldn't understand why Cinderella just hung around and took all that abuse from the stepmother and the stepsisters, why she never fought back.

But she tried to put some enthusiasm into her voice when she opened the book and began to read.

"Once upon a time..."

Fortunately, these kids didn't question Cinderella's wimpiness. She was able to hold their attention all the way till "and they lived happily ever after," and that was when Martin returned with a big bottle of water.

"They're alive!" he exclaimed in delight. "Thanks a lot, Lily."

"You're welcome," she replied. "See you around, Martin. Bye, girls."

She took up her bag and headed toward Rocky Beach. That Martin was a nice guy, she thought, and she wondered where his wife was.

Rocky Beach was deserted, and she climbed up onto the rock she'd found yesterday. She got her notebook out of the bag and opened it. Then she took out her pen and waited for inspiration to strike.

Only nothing happened. She had no idea what she was going to write.

She thought about some of the ideas she'd had the day before. Sierra the mermaid, Sierra the detective... but now she didn't find them appealing. Too silly, too unrealistic. But she couldn't come up with anything to replace them. It was like her head was empty.

Maybe this was what they called "writer's block." But you had to be a writer to have writer's block, and how could she call herself a writer when she hadn't written anything?

Or maybe she couldn't write because she was so hot again. There was no one around, so she left her bag on the rock. Because the ground was covered with rocks, she had to keep her flip-flops on, and when she went into the water, she had to clench her toes to hold them on. It wasn't very comfortable, so she only stayed in for a minute, and then went back to the rock.

Now that she was wet, she couldn't touch her notebook. She made a mental note to bring a towel tomorrow, but for now she had to wait for the sun to dry her off.

While she waited, she took out the iPhone and clicked

on the Contacts icon. There, she entered the only number she knew by heart—her mother's. She labeled it "Mom." Then she texted her mother so Kate would have the number.

She went into the App Store and looked around for some freebies. She downloaded a weather app, Google, and sites that offered different wallpapers and emojis. She tried out a few wallpapers before settling on a unicorn.

Then she found a free Candy Crush game, downloaded it, and played a few rounds. Unfortunately, it was addictive, and she found it hard to stop, even when she knew she was completely dry and it was safe to pick up the notebook.

And then she was too hot again to even think about a story. So she stumbled back across the rocks and into the water, came out, got back on the rock, and played more Candy Crush while she waited to dry off.

This was getting ridiculous, she thought. Maybe if she read for a while, she'd be inspired to write. She took *In Another World* from her bag and opened it.

She'd read a little more last night before going to bed, and found she was actually getting into the story. When she stopped comparing it to Galaxy, she could relax and appreciate the characters and their adventures. And it was so perfect here, curled up on her rock, the soft crashing of the waves in the background...

She was so caught up in the book that she didn't realize she was hungry until she was absolutely starving. She checked her phone for the time, and was startled to see that it was already 3:30.

There hadn't been anything to make a sandwich with at home that morning. So she put the T-shirt on, tossed everything back in her bag. and jumped down from the rock.

Since it was long past lunchtime, there weren't too many people at Chez Betty, which is why she spotted them right away. Those annoying teens were gathered in the center of the terrace at a round table. At least they weren't throwing anything this time.

As she drew closer, she realized there was a new addition to their crew, and she stopped dead in her tracks. Charlotte was with them.

Which was kind of weird, Lily thought. Those kids were older, definitely high school people. Why would they let a middle school girl hang out with them?

She was going to have to pass their table to get to the counter, and she wasn't sure what to do. Ignore them? That would be pretty rude. Maybe just say "hi" to Charlotte and quickly move on.

Charlotte had her back to Lily, so she didn't see her. But one of the boys did. In a high, squeaky voice, he called, "Hello, kitty!"

The others turned in her direction and the girl with pink streaks in her hair started giggling. "My little sister has that shirt. Are you six years old too?"

Charlotte was looking at her now too, and her face was blank, but that wasn't why Lily stared right back at her. Clearly, Charlotte had finally perfected her cat's eye thing, and she'd added hot pink lipstick. Her hair was up in a high ponytail and tied with a scarf. Plus, she must have used one of those fake tan creams, because she was a lot darker than she'd been the night before. Lily knew that Charlotte and her friends back at school wore makeup, but not this much. Charlotte looked as old as the other kids.

"Kind of big for a six-year-old," another boy said. "I'd say she's at least seven. How old are you, little girl?"

"Ooh, she's a shy little girl," Pink Streaks declared. "Hey, little girl, my little sister is on the beach. You want to go play with her?"

Lily was determined to ignore them and move on, but then another boy spoke. "Okay, maybe she's not *physically* six years old. Hey kitty, are you mentally disabled?"

This was too much, she couldn't let that pass. "That's not politically correct," she informed him. "You should say 'intellectually challenged.'"

She was about to add that she was not, but the three boys had already started laughing, and two of the girls joined in. Only Charlotte didn't laugh. And for one brief moment, she thought maybe Charlotte would say "Leave her alone," or "Knock it off," or something like that.

But she didn't, of course. And Lily desperately wanted to

say, "Hey Charlotte, remember me? We share a bedroom." Just to embarrass her in front of these nasty people.

Only she couldn't. Because now her eyes were burning, and she knew what that meant. If she spoke, tears might follow. So she turned away and went to the counter.

Miss Betty recognized her. "Lily, isn't it? Hi there. How's it going?"

"Fine," Lily lied. "Um, can I get a sandwich to go?"

"Sure. There's ham and cheese, chicken and tomato, tuna salad..."

"Tuna salad, please."

"How do you like the cottage?" Miss Betty asked as she wrapped up the sandwich.

"Fine," Lily said again. She really didn't want to get into a conversation about her life so far on Serendipity Bay. She paid for the sandwich, said "Thank you," and took off.

She walked as fast as she could, not just to get away from Charlotte and her friends. But to get back to her rock as quickly as possible.

Because now she knew what she was going to write about.

chapter nine

"Excuse me," Charlotte said. She was feeling flustered, and she didn't want her new friends to see this. "I'll be right back."

She left the table and headed toward the restrooms that were on the side of the café. Her insides were churning, but that was not why she needed to use the facilities. It was Lily again, messing with her head, which then messed up her stomach. Charlotte was doing so well before that stupid girl showed up, wearing that ridiculous T-shirt. Why did she do that? It was like she *wanted* people to make fun of her!

But the memory of Lily's face as they teased her was pretty awful. Still, she deserved it for wearing that shirt, Charlotte told herself.

In the restroom, she checked herself out in the mirror

over the sink. Her makeup was intact, the fake tan looked good, and twisting her hair up had been a brilliant idea.

It had all been going so well for her. When she arrived at the beach in the early afternoon, she spotted them, gathered together on a beach blanket. Pretending not to notice them, she strolled in that direction and paused just by their blanket to take off her sunglasses. And she caught the eye of the boy she'd seen at the restaurant the evening before.

He stared at her for a second, and then said, "Hi."

She looked at him, affected a momentary expression of puzzlement, and then smiled. "Oh, hi. You were at the Barnacle Tavern last night, right?"

"Yeah. Hey, you got a cigarette?"

"No, sorry. Actually, I don't think you're allowed to smoke on the beach." Then, realizing she might have sounded like a prude, she added, "Isn't that ridiculous? I mean, the beach is, like, outside."

He nodded. "Right."

Then, the girl with the spiky cut said, "I'm thirsty. Anyone got water?"

Nobody did, and it was decided they'd go to the café for something to drink. They all began to get up, and the boy turned to Charlotte.

"Wanna come?"

"Okay."

No one else spoke to her as they walked to Chez Betty,

but they weren't giving her bad looks either. Most of the big lunch crowd were gone, so they snagged the round table for six in the center of the terrace.

"Where are you guys from?" she asked the boy.

He named a town that was at least an hour or more from where she lived, which was a relief. It wasn't likely they'd know anyone at her school.

"What about you?" the boy asked.

She told the truth. Unfortunately, the girl with the short hair *did* know someone.

"My cousin lives there. Joey Dale, he's a junior at the high school. You know him?"

She pretended to think. "I'm not sure..."

The guy with the six-pack spoke. "No one knows your cousin, Cassie. He's a total nerd."

Cassie laughed. "True."

Now she knew one name. It was time to get the others. "I'm Charlotte," she offered.

The other names came quickly. She was focused on the guy with the streaked blond hair—his name was Paul. Muscle guy was Jason, and the long-haired dude mumbled something she didn't get. Pink Streaks was Kim.

A waitress came, and they ordered their drinks and a platter of fries to share. Charlotte couldn't take part in a lot of the conversation that ensued—they were talking about people and places she didn't know. Then Jason mentioned a movie she'd actually seen, something about a cosmic empire that she'd liked a lot. Fortunately, she didn't offer her opinion until she heard theirs. They thought it was stupid, so she went along with that.

Everything was moving along perfectly. And then Lily had to show up.

At least she hadn't given Charlotte away. Lily could have greeted her, let the whole table know they were vacationing together, and it would have totally ruined her standing with these kids. She supposed she should feel grateful for that. But grateful to Lily? No, she couldn't feel that.

Back at the table, the group was getting restless.

"Let's get the check and go back to the beach," Cassie said.

Paul looked around. "Hey, I don't see the waitress and nobody's looking. Let's just go."

Charlotte bit her lip. She didn't want to sound prissy around them, but the thought of cheating Miss Betty bothered her. She was taking a risk, but she spoke up.

"Hey guys, you know, they'll figure out we didn't pay and they'll recognize us when we come back. And there's nowhere else to eat or drink around here."

Anxiously, she awaited Paul's reaction. He made a face, but then he shrugged.

"Yeah, okay. The last day we're here, we'll skip out on them."

The others nodded. Charlotte realized that Paul was clearly the unofficial leader of the group, and she basked in his approval of her suggestion.

By the time they were back on the sand kicking a beach ball around, she'd forgotten all about Lily. She was having too good a time and reveling in the fact that high school kids were actually accepting her as one of them. And she was very much aware that every time she looked at Paul, he was looking at her.

He was seriously hot. Not as well-built as Jason, but she'd never been into muscle-bound types. Paul was lean and lanky, his tan made the golden hairs on his arms sparkle, and his eyes were bluer than the ocean. At one point, when they were in the water, the boys started picking up the girls and throwing them back and forth to one another. And when she landed in Paul's arms, she could have sworn he was holding her a lot tighter than necessary.

They were back on the sand as dinnertime was approaching.

"Where are we going tonight?" Kim asked.

"The pizza place," Paul said. He turned to Charlotte. "We're blowing off the families for dinner. Wanna join?"

"I'd better call home first," Charlotte replied. She took her phone out of her bag, and Cassie let out a shriek.

"Is that the new iPhone?"

Thank you, Daddy, she thought as they all admired it and expressed envy. In Contacts, she tapped "Dad."

"Hi Dad. Listen, some friends here on the beach are going out for dinner. Okay if I go?"

"What friends? Is Lily with you?"

She didn't respond to the first question, just the second. "No."

"Well, I'm sorry, honey, but you're not running around town with people I don't even know. Besides, we're barbecuing tonight! I want us all together. This is a family vacation, remember?"

Charlotte's hand tightened on the phone, so tensely that her knuckles were turning white. If it was a family vacation, then why were Kate and Lily there?

But she couldn't start arguing with him, not when all the others could hear. So all she said was "Okay," and disconnected.

"Can't tonight," she told Paul. "We've got visitors."

She wished he would look a little more disappointed. But as they were all getting up and gathering their things, he edged closer to her and spoke softly.

"You're cute."

She gave him what she hoped was a flirtatious look. "You think so?"

"Yes, I do. See you tomorrow?"

"I'll be here," she replied brightly. She waved to the

others and started toward the stairs. Maybe it was better that she couldn't go. She'd be playing hard to get, which, according to what she'd heard, made a girl more desirable.

However, she had no intention of thanking her father for making this possible.

chapter ten

Lily had no idea how much time had passed since she'd returned to Rocky Beach, and she didn't care. This is how real writers must feel, she thought. Nothing else mattered but the story. And this story was practically writing itself. Already, six notebook pages were covered with words.

She'd been writing so furiously and gripping her pen so tightly that her arm was aching. She had to take a break. Closing the notebook and putting the cap back on the pen, she hopped off the rock and stretched. The sun was beating down on her, and the water looked tempting. But if she took a dip, then she'd have to wait until she was dry before she could open the notebook again.

She climbed back onto the rock and decided she'd take a break from writing by looking at what she'd already written. She flipped back to the first page and started reading.

Sierra climbed up the three flights of stairs to the attic. This was where her room was. It was the tiny maid's room at the top of the house.

Sierra wasn't really a maid. She used to have a nice bedroom. But then her father went away, and she was left at home with her stepmother and her stepsister. They made her move up here because they didn't want to look at her.

Lily paused. Someday, when her book was published, Kate might read it. Lily didn't want her to think the evil stepmother was really *her.* Maybe she could describe the character as not looking at all like her mother. She scribbled a note to herself in the margin: *Make stepmother not look like Kate.*

Or maybe there should be an evil step*father.* But she had nothing against John. Maybe she could just leave the adults out altogether. She could write that both the father and his wife were away. Quickly, she made another note in the margin.

But if neither of the parents were evil, then why would Sierra be living in the attic instead of a real bedroom? Why would the stepsister have so much power?

Because... because... maybe they tossed a coin to see who would be in charge when the adults were away, and the stepsister won?

She decided to figure this out later, and continued to read.

Her bedroom was ugly. There was just a mattress on the floor. There was no closet. But that was okay because she didn't have any clothes, except the rags she was wearing.

She heard a loud voice calling her. "Sierra! Come here right now!"

It was the voice of her evil stepsister...

She paused again. She couldn't just keep referring to her as "stepsister"—she needed to give the character a name. But what name? She considered Disney villains—Cruella? Ursula?

No, forget it. She should give her the name she deserved, the name she should have. She took up the pen, and next to "*her evil stepsister,*" she scribbled "*Charlotte.*" Then, scanning the pages, every time she saw "*stepsister,*" she crossed it out and wrote "*Charlotte.*"

She went back to where she left off reading.

Sierra went back down the stairs. She went into Charlotte's bedroom. Charlotte was still in bed, even though it was the afternoon and she wasn't sick or anything.

"What do you want?" Sierra asked her.

"Give me my eyeliner."

"It's right there," Sierra said as she pointed to Charlotte's bureau.

"I don't feel like getting up," Charlotte said. "Bring it to me."

"Why should I?" Sierra asked.

"Because I'm better than you are," Charlotte said. "I'm somebody and you're nobody."

An unfamiliar noise interrupted her, and it took a few seconds before she realized it was her phone. She picked it up and saw that the screen read "Mom."

"Hi Mom."

"Honey, we're getting ready to start up the barbecue. I thought you might want to have a shower and change before dinner."

She *was* feeling pretty sweaty. "Okay, I'm on my way."

"Is Charlotte with you?"

"*No.*"

Kate ignored the emphatic response. "Well, I'll call her on her phone."

Putting the phone back in the bag, Lily hopped off the rock. Then she reconsidered moving too quickly. If her mother was calling Charlotte now, maybe Lily should wait a few minutes to give her a head start, so she wouldn't find herself walking back to the cottage with her.

A sudden wave of depression fell over her. Was this going to be her life for the next two weeks? Arranging everything she did so she wouldn't have to be near Charlotte? And if her mother and Charlotte's father got really serious . . . her life could be changing for a lot longer than two weeks.

She'd been looking forward to the barbecue tonight. Now she wasn't so sure she'd have any appetite.

chapter eleven

In the bathroom, Charlotte scrubbed her face to remove all traces of the heavy makeup, and then applied her usual mascara and lip gloss. She'd lucked out when she'd returned to the cottage—her father and Kate were out in the backyard. She was able to make it into the bathroom without anyone seeing her.

But she needed to come up with a better way of getting the makeup on and off in the days to come. Putting it on wasn't a big problem—she'd just carry a mirror and do her face outside, on her way to the beach. But taking it off... she couldn't count on sneaking into the cottage every day. Tomorrow, she'd go to the village and buy a packet of disposable makeup-remover sheets. Then she could take the stuff off on her way back home.

Of course, at some point her father and Kate would come to

the beach. How could she avoid seeing them there? And what if Lily told them how she was trying to look older? So much to worry about…it was at times like this that she really missed Dahlia. Her mother wouldn't care how much makeup she wore.

Once her face was clean, she took a quick shower, dressed, picked up her phone and speaker, and left the bedroom. Lily was just coming in the front door, but Charlotte pretended not to see her and went out back.

She greeted the adults brightly. "Hi! Did you guys have a good time at the market?"

"It was great," Kate said. "All that farm-fresh food, the most beautiful fruits and vegetables I've ever seen."

"We're going to grill fresh tuna on the barbecue," her father told her.

"Tuna?" In the past, barbecues meant hot dogs and hamburgers, sometimes chicken, sometimes steak. So now they'd be changing their routine for Kate and Lily's pesca-thing.

Kate was looking at her with concern. "You know, Charlotte, I told your father, you two absolutely don't need to follow Lily's and my eating habits."

"It's okay," Charlotte said. "I like tuna. I'm just not used to seeing it on the barbecue."

"But you'd prefer a hamburger?" Kate asked with a smile.

Charlotte couldn't help smiling back. "Sometimes."

"And you'll have them," Kate promised.

Kate was really nice, Charlotte thought. And pretty cool for someone so old. How could she have given birth to a thing like Lily?

She set up her phone and speaker on the picnic table, and got some music going. Her father put her to work shucking corn, and then Lily came out.

"Why don't you help Charlotte with the corn?" Kate suggested.

"Um, I was going to set the table," Lily said.

Kate looked at her daughter meaningfully. "But I think Charlotte could use some help."

"No, I can do it on my own," Charlotte said quickly. She caught the look her father and Kate exchanged, and didn't push it. Neither did Lily.

She sat down on the grass where Charlotte was pulling the silk off the corn.

"You do it like this," Charlotte said.

"I know how to shuck corn," Lily snapped.

They worked silently for a minute. Then Charlotte lowered her voice. "You're not going to say anything to them, are you?"

"About what?"

"*You* know. How I looked on the beach."

"What was so different about how you looked?"

"You couldn't tell that I was wearing makeup?"

Lily shrugged. "I don't notice stuff like that."

She's lying, Charlotte thought. *She doesn't want to admit she paid any attention to me.* But Charlotte couldn't resist a retort. "That figures," she said.

"What's that supposed to mean?" Lily asked, her eyes narrowing.

"You wouldn't know anything about makeup."

"So what? Does that make me weird or something?"

Charlotte needed no time to consider her answer to that. "Yeah. I mean, most girls our age are into makeup. Even if they're not allowed to wear a lot yet, they're *interested.*"

"Well, I'm *not.*"

"So you're not going to tell them?"

"That you're wearing makeup and hanging out with hoodlums?"

"Hoodlums? What are hoodlums?"

"Haven't you ever watched old movies about gangsters? My mother and I love them. That's what they called the criminals back then."

Charlotte looked at her in disbelief. "Are you kidding? They're kids!"

"Okay. Juvenile delinquents. Youthful offenders."

Where did she get these words? "Don't call them that," Charlotte snapped. "They're my friends."

"Okay, so your friends are hoodlums."

"How can you say that? You don't even know them!"

"I saw them throwing French fries yesterday."

"Oh, okay. Throwing French fries. That makes them criminals? Should they go to jail? How about the death penalty?" She hadn't realized their voices were rising until her father called out to them.

"Everything okay over there, girls?"

"Fine," Charlotte called back.

They went back to stripping the corn in silence. Almost unconsciously, Charlotte began singing along with the music coming from the speaker.

"I hate Beyoncé," Lily said.

"Are you nuts? Everybody likes Beyoncé."

"Not me. Can we listen to something else?"

"Like what?"

"Like folk music. Bob Dylan. Or Joan Baez."

Charlotte had heard of them. Her aunt Molly liked that kind of music.

"Nobody our age listens to that stuff."

"*I* do."

"You would."

"Yeah, I guess I'm just special."

Charlotte uttered a short laugh. "Right. As in special ed."

"So now you're saying I'm intellectually challenged? Or what was it your hoodlum friend called me? Mentally disabled?"

"Will you please shut up about my friends?"

"Girls!"

This time it was Kate looking at them worriedly. She looked at John, who shook his head in an "I don't know" way.

"Oh, I almost forgot!" Kate exclaimed. "We got something for you two at the market." She went back into the cottage. She emerged a few seconds later carrying two identical straw tote bags.

"Aren't these cute? They'll be great for carrying stuff back and forth to the beach."

Both girls got up, went over to her, and accepted the bags. "Thank you," they said in unison.

It was actually kind of nice, Charlotte thought as she examined the bag. Light-colored straw, with a blue pattern woven into the design. It would go nicely with her blue bikini.

"Do you like it?" Kate asked.

"Charlotte's waiting to hear if *I* like it," Lily said. "Because if I like it, she'll say she doesn't."

"Lily!" Kate exclaimed.

Charlotte glared at Lily. "That's not true," she responded hotly. "I *do* like it. But I'm just not sure I want to be carrying something *you're* carrying! People might connect us."

"Charlotte!" Her father had joined them. Again, he and Kate shared the same expression, but now it was different. Not worried anymore. Angry.

"I'm getting really sick of this bickering between the two of you!" he declared.

Kate joined in. "I know you two don't hang out together at school, and you're both unique individuals. But surely you can get along! You must have something in common."

"Sorry, Mom, but we don't," Lily replied.

"Thank goodness," Charlotte added.

"That's just not possible," Kate said firmly. "And I suggest that the two of you go to your room and discuss this."

"And don't come out until you find at least one thing you have in common," John ordered. "Or at least something you can agree on."

Charlotte stared at her father in disbelief. Never in her life had he sent her to her room!

Lily looked shocked too. But now, both adults had their arms folded, and the message was clear. Charlotte considered bursting into fake tears, but there was no way she'd lower herself like that in front of Lily. So she turned and headed back toward the cottage. The sound of footsteps behind her told her that Lily was following.

Once they were both in the bedroom, Lily closed the door. Then they each sat down on their own beds. Lily picked up the book on the nightstand, opened it, and started reading. Charlotte turned on her laptop.

But there were no emails to read, and she wasn't in the mood for a game. And after a minute or two, she realized Lily hadn't turned a page in her book. She wasn't really reading.

"This is ridiculous. I'm hungry. And I'm not going to sit in this room forever."

Lily looked up. "Okay, here's what we have in common. We're the same age. We go to the same school. End of story."

Charlotte was silent for a minute. "Do you think they're serious about each other? Your mother and my father?"

Lily shrugged. "I don't know. Maybe. It's the first time she's made a big deal about wanting me to get to know some guy."

Charlotte couldn't remember ever before meeting a woman her father was seeing. "I don't like this," she blurted out. "Your mother's okay, but . . ."

"Yeah, so's your father. But if they get . . ." She seemed to be having a hard time getting the word out, but she finally managed. ". . . if they get *married*, that means you and me . . ."

"Ohmigod," Charlotte breathed. "I know."

She contemplated the possibility, and it was just too terrifying. "We can't let this happen."

Lily nodded. "So we've got something in common. We don't want to live together."

"So what are we going to do about it?" Charlotte wondered aloud. Never in a million years did she think she'd ever use the pronoun "we" in reference to her and Lily. But this situation called for something out of the ordinary.

"We split them up," Lily said. "I mean, make them want to split up."

"How?"

"I don't know."

Charlotte thought about friends back at school who'd had boyfriends and then broke up with them. Usually, it was because either the girl or the boy was into someone else.

"I've got an idea," she said. "Maybe one of them could fall in love with another person."

Lily listened. Her forehead wrinkled, then cleared, and she nodded.

"Yeah, that could work. Okay. And listen—in front of them, we have to act like we're getting along. Because if they're both angry at us, it unites them."

Charlotte agreed. They left the room and went back outside. The adults looked at them anxiously.

"Well?" Charlotte's father asked.

"We found something we have in common," Charlotte said.

"And something we agree about," Lily added.

Kate's eyebrows went up. "Really? What?"

The girls looked at each other.

"It's kind of private," Lily said.

Charlotte nodded. "Personal stuff. Is that okay?"

"Sure," her father said. "As long as it means you two can get along."

He was looking pretty pleased with himself, Charlotte thought. So was Kate. If only they knew what she and Lily had in mind.

But now her father was happily throwing tuna steaks on the barbecue, and Kate was fixing a salad. The girls gathered up the ears of corn and brought them to the grill. Minutes later, they all sat down on the picnic bench to eat. And while the girls didn't get into any real conversation with each other, they listened to the parents and joined in with whatever they talked about. Afterward, they cleaned up and did the dishes together. Then Kate and John went for a walk on the beach.

Lily got her notebook and said she was going outside to write. "It helps me to get ideas if I write them down," she said.

"Okay," Charlotte said. She already had an idea. In the bedroom, she opened her laptop and went into the email.

Hi Mom. How are you? I'm not so good. I'm missing you a lot.

chapter twelve

Having made a pact with Charlotte wasn't going to suddenly turn them into BFFs, Lily was certain of that. Still, the atmosphere in their room the next morning did seem a little less tense. Charlotte even asked her for a favor.

She had put on a light blue bikini and was examining herself critically in the mirror.

"Could you move the hook on the back of my top to the next loop?"

"It looks okay now," Lily said.

"I know, but if it's tighter, it'll make my boobs look bigger."

It was on the tip of Lily's tongue to say something like "they're already big enough," but she managed to restrain herself. Gingerly, she unhooked and rehooked Charlotte's bikini top.

"Thanks."

Now she felt like she had to make some effort at conversation. "About last night...have you come up with any ideas?"

"Yeah," Charlotte said. "What about you?"

"Sort of. Maybe." If Charlotte wasn't going to share her idea, then neither would she. Besides, she wasn't even sure yet if her idea was a real possibility. There was something she had to find out first.

That was pretty much the extent of the conversation. At the breakfast table, with the watchful parents there, they managed a few words along the lines of "Could you pass the juice, please?" and "Thank you," and "You're welcome." John and Kate seemed satisfied.

"Are you guys going to the beach today?" Charlotte asked.

"I'm not really a beach person," Kate said. "I burn so easily. But we'll probably take a stroll over there later."

"When?" Charlotte asked. "What time?"

Kate looked puzzled. "I'm not sure... why?"

"I was just curious," Charlotte said quickly.

But Lily could guess why she'd asked. She didn't want her father and Kate to see her wearing a ton of makeup and hanging with those older kids. Of course, despite what she'd said to Charlotte, she'd noticed the girl's appearance. She just hadn't wanted Charlotte to think she'd even looked at her.

She wondered how the girl would deal with the inevitable appearance of the parents on the beach. Charlotte couldn't hang out at Chez Betty—they were bound to stop by there. Would she stay in the water all day? Lily didn't really care what she did. Her only concern was that the adults' united concern about Charlotte might bring them closer.

The girls, both carrying their identical straw totes, left the cottage together. But as soon as they were some distance from the cottage, Charlotte stopped and ducked behind a palm tree. She sat down on the ground, took a little bag from her tote, and dumped out the contents—tubes, wands, compacts, a mirror.

"You go on," she instructed Lily.

Lily understood. Charlotte wouldn't want them to be seen arriving at the beach together, especially not with identical totes. And Lily had no interest in watching Charlotte put on her makeup. Still, she had to say something.

"I'm leaving, but just for your information, it's not because I'm taking orders from you. I don't want to be associated with you any more than you want to be associated with me."

"Fine," Charlotte replied. "But don't forget our plan."

She wouldn't, it was way too important. There was no way on earth she'd spend the rest of her life with Charlotte Nettles.

Reaching the beach, Lily stood at the top of the stairs

and scanned the area. She went down, and crossed the sand past the jetty to Rocky Beach.

Once in position on her special rock, with her notebook open and pen in hand, she considered what she'd write today. She still wasn't sure what to do about the adult characters in her novel. Maybe she was trying too hard to imitate Cinderella. She certainly didn't want Sierra to be a constant victim. She decided that for now, she would just concentrate on the battles between the two girls, and figure out how to connect them later.

She went back to the scene in Charlotte's bedroom and started writing.

"Bring me my eyeliner," Charlotte screamed. "Now!"

Sierra didn't pick up the eyeliner. Instead, she picked up a pillow from the bed. She pushed it down onto Charlotte's face. Charlotte struggled, but Sierra just pushed harder. Harder and harder, until Charlotte stopped moving.

She stopped. Maybe this was a little too violent. Besides, she couldn't kill off the villain this early in the story. She didn't tear out the page or cross out what she'd written, though—she'd save it for later.

She turned the page and started writing another scene.

Sierra was mopping the floor. Just then, Charlotte and her hoodlum friends walked in.

"What a funny-looking maid!" the girl with pink streaks in her hair said. "She's dressed in rags!"

"I am not the maid," Sierra said. "I live here too."

"No, she doesn't," Charlotte said. "She's nobody. Just some dirty thing who hangs around."

Sierra picked up the bucket of water and dumped it on Charlotte's head. "Who's dirty now?" she asked as she laughed.

Funny, how good it felt to write stuff like this! It was almost as good as doing it in real life.

The ideas were coming faster now, and she wrote rapidly. Somehow Sierra figures out Charlotte's password and changes her music preferences to folk music. Sierra Photoshop's Charlotte's head on the body of a woman covered with tattoos and posts it on Instagram. Sierra puts an announcement on Charlotte's Facebook page, saying that she's become a bird-watcher. Or a chess player. Something Charlotte's crowd would consider very uncool.

And the best one so far: Charlotte is in the bath. Sierra texts Charlotte's friends and tells them to come over. She steals all of Charlotte's clothes and leaves behind only a certain, specially selected top. Then she sets off the fire alarm. Charlotte can either run out of the house stark naked or wearing a Hello Kitty T-shirt. Either way, everyone would be laughing at her.

This is good, she thought. The book was going well. But she had to stop—she was hungry. She'd packed a sandwich and fruit that morning, so she didn't need to go to Chez Betty and risk a barrage of insults.

When she finished eating, Lily realized she didn't much feel like going on with her novel at the moment. Maybe all that writing had burned out her anger. She wasn't worried, though. Another evening with Charlotte would give her fuel. Anyway, it was now time to go check out the main beach.

There was no sign of Charlotte and her friends, but she spotted someone she was actually pleased to see—that nice man, Martin, and his little girls. As she drew closer, she saw that the twins were piling up mounds of sand, and Martin was reading.

"Hi, I hope I'm not disturbing you," she said.

Martin looked up from his book. "Not at all!" He indicated the book he was now closing. "It's a mystery, and I think I already know who did the bad deed."

"I hate when that happens," Lily commented.

"Yeah, but I still have to finish it to know if I'm right. You like mysteries?"

Lily nodded. "But I really love fantasies more. Like the Rulers of the Galaxy series."

"Terrific books," Martin said with approval.

Lily's eyes widened. She'd never met an adult who knew those books. "Have you seen the TV series too?"

"Absolutely, and I think it's as good as the books. Maybe even better."

"I think so too!" Lily exclaimed. "Who's your favorite character?"

"Darius," Martin replied promptly.

"Mine too! But I think they're all pretty great. Like, in the books, I was never much interested in Mortune—you know, the one with the pointy nose. But he's just about my favorite character in the show. After Darius, of course."

"That actor is amazing," Martin agreed.

At that moment, a wail went up from Rose—or maybe it was Sarah. Lily couldn't remember which one had the freckle.

"What's the matter?" Martin asked.

"It won't stay up!" the child cried. She put a fistful of sand on top of the mound, and the grains trickled down the side.

"Are you building a castle?" Lily asked.

Two heads bobbed up and down.

"Then you need water, that's what makes it stick. Wait, I'll show you." She took an empty bucket, went down to the water's edge and filled it. Returning to the girls, she poured a little water onto the mound of sand.

"See, now you can mold it to make a castle."

The girls watched in awe. They caught on right away, and soon they were happily at work.

Martin was watching. "Thanks, Lily. I should have shown them that. Sometimes I think I'm a terrible father!"

"Oh, I'm sure you're a great father," Lily said. *But where is the mother?* she wondered again. "It can't be easy, being all by yourself with them," she ventured.

"Mm. And I'm not really used to it." He glanced at the girls and lowered his voice. "My... my partner and I just recently split up."

"Oh. I'm sorry to hear that."

"Well, it was for the best."

Actually, she wasn't sorry at all. In fact, learning that Martin was eligible made her heart leap. He was perfect! He looked to be around the same age as her mother. He was nice, he was a reader. And if he liked Rulers, he had to be pretty smart.

He was gazing out at the sea, and suddenly he exclaimed, "Wow, look at that!"

In the distance, a surfer was sailing on the crest of a wave, with a girl balancing on his shoulders. Martin quickly reached into his bag, pulled out a camera, and started snapping photos.

Lily gasped. "Are you a photographer?"

"No, it's only a hobby. But I love photography."

She knew it was forward of her, but she couldn't resist asking. "What do you do for a living?"

"I'm just a dull, ordinary lawyer."

A lawyer—more good news. Lawyers made money. Not that Kate would ever be into a guy just because he was rich. But it would be so nice if she could concentrate on her arty photographs and stop taking wedding pictures.

Of course, John made a lot of money as a businessman.

But John came with Charlotte. Martin came with Sarah and Rose. And Lily wouldn't mind a couple of little sisters.

"Daddy, can we go in the water now?" one of them asked.

Martin looked longingly at his book.

"I'll take them," Lily offered. It certainly wouldn't hurt to show him how helpful an older sister could be. "Really, I'm a good swimmer. I won't take them to where it's over their heads, and we'll stay where you can see them."

"Girls, you want to go in the water with Lily?" Martin asked.

"Yes!" they chorused.

Lily helped them put on their water wings, took each one by a hand, and walked them to the water.

"Let's jump in the waves," she suggested.

The twins jumped up and down and squealed with pleasure.

"My name is Rose," said the one with the freckle. "And your name is Lily. We're flowers!" She turned to her sister. "You're not a flower."

An ominous expression came onto the other twin's face.

"Yes she is," Lily said. "She's a Sarah. That's the name of an imaginary flower."

"What does it look like?" Sarah asked.

"It's pink. Pink and..."

"Yellow!" Sarah yelled.

"Yes, pink and yellow. And it smells like chocolate!"

When the girls tired of jumping and began begging to go deeper into the water, Lily suggested they hunt for shells. A little while later they returned to Martin to show off the treasures they'd gathered.

It was while he was admiring them that she saw her mother coming down the stairs to the beach.

"I'll be right back," she said, and ran to meet her.

"Hi Mom, where's John?"

"He's on a conference call with his office, he'll be along soon. Where's Charlotte?"

"Oh, she's around somewhere," Lily said. She couldn't believe her luck, having her mother here by herself. "Come on, there's someone I want you to meet."

She led Kate to Martin and the girls.

"Martin, this is my mother, Kate Holden."

Martin rose. He was even polite! "Hi, I'm Martin Barrow."

"That's Rose and Sarah," Lily said, pointing. Then, to Martin, she said, "My mother's a professional photographer."

Martin was clearly impressed. "Really? I was just telling Lily how much I like photography."

"Have you seen the exhibit at the Westbrook Museum?" Kate asked him.

"Not yet, but I'm planning to go when I get back home."

"Do you live near the museum?" Lily asked.

It turned out that Martin lived in the next town over from their own. This was getting too unbelievably good for words.

He nodded toward the girls. "Of course, with these two, it's hard for me to get out much."

"I could babysit!" Lily offered.

Her mother looked at her strangely. Lily had never shown any interest in babysitting.

But then Martin engaged Kate in a discussion of cameras, and Lily joined the twins, who were back to building sandcastles. Every time she glanced at her mother and Martin, they were talking.

So excellent, so absolutely perfect. They even looked good together.

And if her luck held, maybe Charlotte had already found someone for her father too.

chapter thirteen

Charlotte had always liked roaming around the area everyone jokingly called "Downtown Dipity." It was kind of like an old-fashioned Main Street—one pharmacy, one grocery store, a beauty salon, and a couple dozen cute shops. Plus, there were street stalls, where local artists and craftspeople displayed their stuff. It wasn't like going to the Mall back home, but Charlotte usually found *something* to buy—a cute pair of earrings made of seashells, or a hand-painted scarf.

She'd made this walk a zillion times, since she was a tiny kid, holding her parents' hands. Now, strolling along with Paul, Kim, and Jason, she was pleased when several merchants recognized her and greeted her warmly. She kind of hoped it would impress her friends.

Paul was more impressed with a display of key rings,

decorated with strange charms. He was particularly interested in one that had a massive plastic skull dangling from it.

"This would be so cool for the bike keys," he declared.

"When are you getting it?" Jason asked.

"My brother's heading in tonight. Oh man, wait till you see this monster. It's a massive Harley, dual disc brakes, rear suspension..."

By now, Charlotte had realized he wasn't talking about a bicycle.

Jason was clearly in awe. "And he's really going to let you take it out? On your own?"

Paul grinned. "'Course I had to bribe him. Fifty bucks for three full days with the bike."

Charlotte took out her phone. She'd been checking email periodically, expecting to hear from her mother. That email she'd sent her demanded an immediate response. But she'd forgotten to plug it in the evening before, and the battery was dead.

Kim nudged her. "Check out those amazing beach cover-up things over there."

Charlotte looked in the direction Kim indicated. Outside the store, there was a rack of flashy sarongs and flowered tunics. Not Charlotte's taste at all—in fact, she thought they were hideous. But if Kim liked them...

"Yeah, they're cute."

"Are you crazy?" Kim yelped. "They're so ugly!"

Charlotte recovered quickly. "I was being sarcastic."

"Oh, okay!"

With no water to jump into, the heat was becoming unbearable. "Let's get ice cream," Charlotte suggested.

"I don't know, babe," Paul said. "I'm a little short of funds. I have to hold on to my stash to bribe my brother."

"My treat," Charlotte declared. Her father had given her some money that morning. She was supposed to be using it to have lunch with Lily.

Now Paul *really* looked impressed. "So you're a rich kid, huh?"

Charlotte tossed her hair charmingly and uttered a tinkling laugh. "Hardly. I raided my father's wallet this morning." Which made it sound like she swiped the money, which wasn't true. But if she was using the money for something that wasn't what it was supposed to be used for—then maybe it was true. In any case, she was pleased with the expressions of approval on the others' faces.

"I do that all the time," Kim told her.

They started to cross the street to Serendipity Dip when suddenly a burly man grabbed Paul by the shoulder.

"I saw you take that key chain," the man barked. "Pay up now or I'm calling the cops."

Paul didn't appear to be the least bit concerned. "First of all, I didn't steal any key chain. Secondly, are you really going to call the police for something that probably cost what . . . five bucks?"

"Ten," the man said. "And that's not the point. I don't care if it cost two cents, you don't take something without paying for it." He fingered a whistle that hung from his neck on string. "See this? I blow it and a cop will be here in three seconds."

Paul grinned. "Do it. Or search me yourself. You ain't going to find anything." He extended his arms, just like the police demanded suspects do on TV.

To Charlotte's surprise, the man *did* pat him down, then demanded that Paul empty his pockets. There was nothing in them but his wallet and his phone.

He then checked Jason's pockets and ordered the girls to open their bags. That was when he found the key chain with the plastic skull charm—in Charlotte's embroidered tote.

She gasped. She didn't have to fake any shock, it was very real. "Ohmigod, I don't know how that got in there!"

"Sure you don't," the man said, the sarcasm practically dripping from his lips.

She glanced at Paul. Now he was actually looking nervous. And then she knew what he'd done.

She thought quickly. "I was looking at it," she lied. "And it must have dropped in . . . I'm so sorry. How much did you say it was?"

Her heart was beating so rapidly, for a minute she thought she might faint. But the man just scowled, took the money, and went back to his stall.

"You are one cool chick," Paul said.

She offered up an uneasy smile. She'd never been into shoplifting. Some friends at school picked stuff up in stores occasionally—a lipstick, something small like that. It seemed kind of silly to Charlotte—they could all afford to buy the stuff. Besides, it just didn't feel right. Still, she never said anything to her friends about it, and she wasn't about to say anything to Paul.

And she was rewarded for this. He tossed an arm loosely around her shoulders, and they walked like this into the ice cream parlor.

She was still shaking a little as they stood in line to order their cones. She paid for all of them, and had only a dime left. Back outside, Paul started talking to Jason and Kim pulled her aside.

"He likes you," she whispered.

"Paul?"

Kim nodded. "And not just because you saved his butt. I can tell, from the way he looks at you. Cassie's gonna be so jealous. She's been into him for, like, forever."

"Well, I'm glad she's not here then," Charlotte said lightly.

"You two need some time alone," Kim declared. She raised her voice. "Hey Jason, didn't you say you wanted to get a haircut?"

"Oh yeah, that's right," he replied.

"I'll come with you," Kim said.

They took off. Paul returned his arm to Charlotte's

shoulders, and they walked in the other direction. She was still feeling a little weird about the whole key-chain business, but it was so nice strolling along the street with a gorgeous guy by her side. She wished she could do a selfie to post so her friends could see this.

Paul's phone rang, and he took it out of his pocket.

"Yeah? Hi, Mom. Oh, okay. Yeah, I'll be right there. Bye."

He turned to Charlotte. "My older brother just showed up. I gotta go do the 'so happy to see you' bit."

"Your parents won't mind if you use his bike?"

He shook his head. "They won't know. They're going away for a couple of days. That's why my brother's here." He grinned. "They don't trust me with the kid."

Charlotte remembered a young boy at the table with Paul and his parents at the restaurant.

"I don't blame them," she said teasingly. "You might make him help you rob a bank."

He laughed. "That reminds me . . . you don't really want to keep that key chain, do you?"

She forced a laugh. "Not my style," she said. She went into her tote and took out the key chain.

He took it. Then he put *both* arms around her and kissed her. Right on the lips. And it wasn't just a peck. It *lasted.*

"See you at the beach," he said, when he finally released her. "Maybe tonight?"

She didn't walk back to the cottage—she floated. She

was pleased to find the place empty when she arrived—she'd completely forgotten to take her makeup off. Plus, she wanted time alone, to think about Paul and his kiss.

After washing her face, she remembered that she still hadn't seen her email. Dahlia could be coming at any moment. Though that was probably just wishful thinking.

She opened her PC and logged in. There was a note from Ashley, an announcement of a sale at Victoria's Secret, and a demand to renew her subscription to digital *Teen Vogue*. Nothing from her mother.

But she wasn't as depressed as she thought she would be. Now, she was thinking about tonight at the beach. With Paul. And more kisses.

chapter fourteen

Lily hurried into the cottage. In the bedroom, she found Charlotte sitting at the little vanity table smiling at herself in the mirror.

"Did you find someone for your father?"

"No."

Then what did she look so happy about, Lily wondered. "Well, I've kept *my* end of the bargain."

"What do you mean?"

She told Charlotte about Martin. "He's perfect for her."

"That's nice," Charlotte murmured.

Lily frowned. Charlotte was acting like she'd completely forgotten about their deal.

"You'd better get to work," she warned her. "When Mom breaks up with him, your father will be miserable. And I like your father. I don't want him to be depressed."

Charlotte sighed, but she finally tore her eyes from her reflection.

"I *am* working on it. I wrote my mother."

"But they're divorced, right?"

"So what? There's no law that says divorced people can't remarry. And deep down inside, I know they still love each other. I just need to get them together."

"Do you think she'll come here?"

"Well, I wrote her that I was feeling kind of down."

Lily approved. "Good move." Surely any mother would respond to that. "What would be perfect is if they both find themselves in love with someone else at the same time. That way, no one suffers."

Charlotte nodded. "And you and I don't ever have to speak to each other again."

They heard the cottage door open, and Lily went out to greet Kate and John. Their arms were full of grocery bags.

"Another cookout tonight!" Kate announced as Lily took one of the bags. "With company this time."

"Who?"

"Your friend Martin and his daughters."

Lily almost dropped the bag. This was happening even faster than she thought it could. Of course, with John here, nothing romantic could start. At least, nothing obvious. But sparks could still start flying. She just hoped John wouldn't notice.

"What did you get?" Lily asked as they all dropped their bags on the kitchen counter.

"Something for everyone," John told her. He was looking very cheerful. Turning to Kate, he said, "I'm sorry, darling, but I do need my meat once in a while."

Kate gave him a peck on the cheek. "No problem, my dear. I told you, I won't inflict my habits on you."

Lily observed this little interaction with concern. *Darling. My dear.* They really had affection for each other. But she brushed her fears aside. They could still have more affection for someone else.

"Go have your shower now," Kate told John. "Lily will help me unload this stuff."

They began putting things away, and Kate recited the evening's menu.

"Burgers for John, Charlotte, and Martin. Hot dogs for Sarah and Rose. Eggplant for you and me. Corn on the cob again, for everyone. And I'm making your favorite macaroni salad."

So Martin wasn't a vegetarian. Too bad. But it was interesting that her mother already knew the twins' names. That had to mean something.

Lily could hear the shower now, but even so she lowered her voice. "Martin's really cool, isn't he?"

"Very nice guy," Kate agreed.

"Great sense of humor."

"Mm."

"And those little girls are so cute. Really well-behaved. No trouble at all."

Her mother handed her stalks of celery. "Could you start chopping these for the macaroni salad?"

Lily picked up a knife. "Good-looking too."

"What?"

"Martin. He's very good-looking, don't you think?"

Her mother nodded, but she didn't seem to be listening. "Where are the onions?" she murmured to herself as she searched through one of the bags. "Oh, here they are."

John, freshly showered and dressed, reappeared and began molding the ground beef into patties. And Lily went to grab the shower before Charlotte took it over.

When she came out—only five minutes later—Charlotte was standing by the bathroom door, tapping her foot and looking impatient. Which was very annoying, when you considered the fact that *she* spent at least twenty minutes in there when she showered.

"Look, I'm going to sneak out tonight," Charlotte said. "And you're not going to say anything, right?"

Lily couldn't resist. "Meeting your hoodlums at the beach?"

Charlotte almost smiled. "Just one of them."

Lily just rolled her eyes and went to the bedroom. She wanted to look good in front of Martin, like someone he'd be proud to call a daughter. Of course, it wouldn't make any real difference as to how he would react. He was bound to fall in love with Kate no matter what Lily looked like, but Lily came with Kate, and she wanted Martin to appreciate the whole package.

So for once, she was glad that Charlotte was spending forever in the shower, so Lily could go through the sparse wardrobe she'd brought with her to Serendipity Bay and pick out the best thing possible. No funny T-shirts tonight—she chose the little flowered sundress her mother had tossed into her bag just in case they went out somewhere nice.

After that, she started tidying the living room, rearranging the throw pillows, straightening the pictures on the walls.

Her mother walked in. "What are you doing?"

"I just want everything to look nice. Is that what you're going to wear?"

Kate always looked pretty, but her denim skirt was wrinkled.

"Why?" she asked. "Isn't this okay?"

"Oh, sure. I was just remembering that pink striped dress you brought. You haven't worn it at all."

Kate looked at her curiously, and Lily wasn't surprised. When was the last time she'd noticed what her mother was wearing? To avoid any questions, she announced, "I'll set the table outside," and left the room.

In the yard, John was getting the barbecue started up.

"Don't you look lovely!" he said when he saw her. "What's the occasion?" Then he caught himself. "I mean, you look lovely all the time, I just haven't seen you in a dress before."

Lily laughed. "Oh, I just felt like dressing up. 'Cause we're having company."

John pretended to pout. "You mean you wouldn't dress up just for me?" Then he smiled. "Actually, I'm glad of that. I wouldn't want you to think of me as company."

He really was so sweet, Lily thought. She couldn't help feeling a little guilty about the scheme to separate him from her mother. She hoped Charlotte was right, that he still really loved his ex-wife. Like they said, all's fair in love and war. Maybe her war with Charlotte could end up with both parents finding true love.

When Martin and his kids arrived, Lily watched anxiously as Kate introduced them to John. He didn't seem the least bit perturbed by the fact that his girlfriend had invited a handsome single guy to their cookout. They shook hands, and at first they made polite nice-to-meet-you talk, about the weather, the beach, that sort of stuff. Then it turned out that they knew someone in common—one of Martin's lawyer colleagues represented someone at John's company, and the conversation became more lively.

Lily occupied herself with Rose and Sarah. She liked the twins, but like on the beach, she wanted Martin to see what kind of big sister she could be. They tossed a ball around, and then, using a clothesline as a net, she showed them some rudimentary volleyball moves.

Charlotte finally emerged. She too had dressed up a little—she wore a short ruffled skirt with a midriff-baring halter. When she joined Lily and the twins in their game, Lily was surprised—and then she realized this was all part of the show, to let the parents think they were getting along. But when one of the twins asked, "Are you sisters?" in unison Charlotte and Lily responded with a resounding "No!"

Dinner went well. Lily kept her eyes on her mother and Martin, watching for sparks. Kate hadn't changed her clothes, but it didn't matter, she couldn't help looking great. At one point, Martin told a joke that had Kate doubled over laughing. But John was laughing too, and he didn't look the least bit jealous.

For someone who was into meat, Charlotte barely touched her hamburger, and she kept looking at her watch. Then, just as John was bringing out a tart for dessert, she touched her head and uttered what Lily thought was a very unconvincing groan.

"I've got a headache," she said.

But before anyone could respond to that, there was a call from inside the cottage. "Hello? Anyone home?"

A second later, a woman came out into the yard. She looked like a model, someone who'd just stepped out of the

pages of a fashion magazine—tall, slender, golden hair, little black dress, stiletto heels.

Lily felt suddenly sick. Was this Martin's wife, or girlfriend—the "partner" he'd referred to? But from the look on Charlotte's face—a combination of total surprise and enormous joy—she realized that this woman wasn't Martin's wife or girlfriend or partner.

She was someone else's ex-wife. And Charlotte's mother.

chapter fifteen

When Charlotte woke up the next morning, for a few seconds she had no idea where she was. All she knew was that she was enveloped by sheets that felt like silk, and her head was on a pillow that felt like it was stuffed with feathers.

Opening her eyes, she saw walls covered in pale yellow, sleek modern furniture, windows shaded by gauzy curtains. Then she remembered she was in a hotel—not *any* hotel, *the* hotel, the fanciest one in Serendipity Bay, the hotel with the private beach. This was where her mother was staying, in a suite with a living room and two bedrooms.

She lay very still, enjoying the luxury of the huge bed and thinking back to the evening before.

Dahlia had looked so incredibly beautiful when she'd stepped out into the backyard. That chic dress, the huge

gold earrings—how she must have looked next to Kate, in her wrinkled denim skirt and tank top, and with her sunburned nose. She wished she'd thought to look at her father to catch his reaction. In all honesty, she had to admit that Kate was a pretty woman, but compared to Dahlia—well, there was no comparison.

Her mother had swooped in like an exotic bird, kissing the cheeks of each person she was introduced to. And then she'd announced that she'd come to collect her darling daughter.

Charlotte had run to her room to pack up a few things and they'd taken off.

"I'm so glad you're here," she'd told Dahlia as they taxied to the hotel. "I didn't know if you could come."

"But of course we came!" Dahlia had said.

Charlotte's heart had sunk. *We.* So she wasn't here alone.

Dahlia had gone on. "And it worked out really well, since Jay's got a meeting with a music-industry big shot in the area."

Charlotte had felt her heart drop even lower. She hadn't just come for her daughter.

At least she hadn't had to meet Jay right away. He was still jet-lagged, her mother had explained, and was still sleeping. When they arrived at the hotel, they went to the cocktail lounge, where Dahlia ordered some little fancy appetizer things and a bottle of white wine. Charlotte had just wanted a soft drink, but her mother insisted she have a little wine too.

"You know, traveling in Europe, I saw young people no older than you drinking wine."

"Really?" She had taken a sip, and as usual, she had tried to look like she enjoyed it.

"We had such a marvelous time, I can't wait to take you there. Jay's band is about to sign with a major recording label. It's just a fabulous coincidence that an executive from the company has a summer house near here. They're going to cut an album, and once it's released we'll be touring again. Only this time, you'll come with us. For months and months, all around the world!"

"I've got school," Charlotte had reminded her, but Dahlia brushed that off.

"School! Charlotte, *travel* is an education. Oh, darling, what I've seen!"

That set her off on a description of London, Paris, Rome... Charlotte had only half listened. She had been trying to figure out how she could get her parents alone, together.

When her mother had paused for a breath, Charlotte had broken in. "How long are you staying here?"

"We have a flight tomorrow evening."

"You're only here for one day?" Charlotte had asked in dismay.

"Jay's meeting the band at a studio, to start work on the

album." She had lowered her voice to a dramatic whisper. "Don't tell anyone, but once they've finished recording this album, he thinks he might go solo. That's why he wants to meet with the big shot privately."

Like I care, Charlotte had thought. "But do you have to go too? Can't you stay a little longer?"

"Darling, that's impossible, Jay would have a fit! I'm his muse, you know. He needs me for inspiration." She leaned forward and clutched Charlotte's hand. "Now, tell me all about *you*! What's going on? Have you met any cute boys this summer?"

Suddenly, Charlotte had remembered Paul. He could have been on the beach right then, looking for her. Maybe playing hard to get would just increase his interest. But getting her parents together was more important.

"Well, there's this one boy," she began, but her mother had suddenly put a hand to her own mouth in a futile effort to stop a yawn.

"I'm so sorry, darling, I'm just exhausted, I still haven't recovered from the jet lag. Don't worry, we've got all day tomorrow to talk and catch up."

And now, it was tomorrow, and Charlotte couldn't afford to waste any more time lying in bed. Her mother was leaving tonight, and she had to move fast. If only some sort of brilliant idea would hit her. She almost wished Lily was there, to help her come up with a plan. She had to admit, her finding that cute guy for Kate so quickly had been brilliant.

She dressed quickly and went through the door that led into the living room of the suite. No one was there, and the door to her mother's bedroom was open. No one was in there either. Then she saw a note on the coffee table.

Come downstairs to the restaurant for breakfast.

There were a lot of people in the elegant restaurant, but she spotted her mother immediately. Dahlia stood out, her golden hair piled up in a messy bun, and wearing a long, gold caftan. She wasn't alone.

The man sitting across from her wore huge sunglasses that practically covered his face, but Charlotte recognized the silly dreadlocks from the video she'd watched. Slowly, she made her way to the table.

Dahlia spotted her and waved. "Darling!" she cried out in a voice that was just a little too loud. "Come meet Jay!"

He didn't stand up—he didn't even remove his sunglasses. He just nodded and mumbled, "Hi, kid."

Her mother pointed to the buffet. "Go get some breakfast, darling, and hurry back here!"

Like there was somewhere else she would go? She went to the buffet, a long table covered with delectable goodies. She wished she was hungrier. She picked up a couple of croissants and some orange juice.

Returning, she saw her mother and Jay leaning across the

table and kissing. Smooching, actually. Their faces were plastered together, and people were looking at them. Charlotte wasn't sure she'd even be able to choke down the croissants.

At least they stopped when she sat down.

"Now, darling, tell me why you're feeling so low."

So low? Charlotte looked at her blankly. Then she remembered what she'd written in the email.

"Oh. Well, it's sort of complicated..."

"Is it the boy?"

"The boy?"

"You said last night, you met a boy."

"No, it's not that. Mom..." she glanced quickly in the direction of Jay. The man was concentrating on his food, but there was no way she could talk to her mother in front of him.

"It's kind of personal."

"Oh darling, you can say anything to Jay! He's going to be family!"

"What do you mean?"

Dahlia lifted her left hand and wiggled her fingers. How had Charlotte missed seeing the diamond the night before? It was certainly big enough.

"We're engaged, darling! Jay is going to be your stepfather!"

chapter sixteen

Rose and Sarah shrieked in delight as Lily lifted them, one at a time, and gently dropped them into the crest of an oncoming wave.

The little girls were wearing water wings, so they bobbed in the foam. It was low tide, so even if their feet hit the ground they wouldn't go underwater. Still, Lily kept her eyes on them, only glancing away every now and then to check out the couple on the beach. Her mother and Martin, sitting side by side, seemed to be in deep conversation.

John wasn't with them. He'd had some kind of important Skype call scheduled, so he'd stayed at the cottage.

Lily immediately saw that this worked to everyone's advantage. She'd sent a text to Charlotte, alerting her that her father would be alone. Kate and Martin could connect without interference. And Charlotte could bring her mother to the cottage, where John and his ex-wife could renew their love.

Everything was falling into place and coming along so nicely. She imagined a group conversation that would take place very soon, maybe even tonight. John and her mother would gently tell her and Charlotte that they were ending this relationship, that it was on good terms, that they both agreed to it, that they would remain friends, blah, blah, blah. She and Charlotte would fake a little dismay, and that would be the end of it.

She wondered if Martin's cottage was big enough to take them in. If not, this would mean the premature end to her vacation. Which was too bad—she liked Serendipity Bay. Still, it was worth the sacrifice of a vacation if it meant not having Charlotte in her life.

"My turn! My turn!"

"Oh, right." She lifted Rose and tossed her. Then she glanced back at Kate and Martin. They were laughing now. She remembered overhearing her mother once tell a friend that she always fell in love with men who made her laugh.

Finally, both twins started shivering, and they barely protested when Lily led them out of the water. She settled them on a blanket in front of Martin, and her mother rose.

"I'm going to pick up some sandwiches for everyone at Chez Betty. Come help me, Lily?"

"Sure." She was dying for a few minutes alone with her

mother anyway. Maybe she'd get a hint of how things were progressing with Martin.

Walking to the café, she brought him up right away. "Isn't Martin just the best?"

Her mother obliged with warm words. "He's a great guy. Very funny! And I'm curious to see what kind of photographer he is. We're planning to get together after this vacation so I can look at his work."

Lily restrained herself from hopping up and down. "I just knew you two would hit it off!" she exclaimed happily. Emboldened, she continued. "You make a cute couple."

"What?"

"You and Martin! You look good together, you have the same sense of humor, you're both into photography—it's a perfect match!"

Her mother stopped walking. "Lily, what on earth are you talking about?"

"Come on, Mom. You just said you like him. And I can tell he likes you."

Her mother looked at her in bewilderment. Then she smiled softly, and shook her head. "Oh no, Lily. Not in that way."

"How can you be so sure?" Lily challenged her.

"Honey... Martin's gay."

Lily stared at her in disbelief. It took a moment for the words to penetrate.

"No, Mom, no way!" she blurted out. "That's not true! Martin can't be gay!"

"Of course he can! And why are you so shocked? You know gay people."

"But…but…" She struggled for words. "He's got children!" Even as she said that, she knew it was meaningless. And so did her mother.

"Now, Lily, you know better than that. Lots of gay couples have children. Martin and his ex-partner, they separated amicably, and now they have joint custody of the twins."

They'd reached the counter at Chez Betty, and Kate gave their order. While they waited, Lily couldn't think of anything to say. She felt like her whole world had just crumbled.

Her mother saw this. "You're upset! Why?" Then realization must have hit her. "Oh, Lily. Were you trying to fix Martin and me up?"

Lily nodded.

"But…I'm with John, honey. And you like him." Her forehead puckered. "Don't you?"

"Oh, sure. John's cool. It's just…"

"Just what?" Her face darkened. "Charlotte? But you two seem to be getting along better."

What could she say? That it was all an act, that they still positively despised each other?

The sandwiches were produced, Kate paid for them, and they started back. Halfway there, Lily stopped.

"I'm going to take a walk."

"But we're going to eat now."

"I'm not hungry." And she started toward Rocky Beach. She could almost feel her mother's eyes still on her, watching her worriedly, but she didn't look back.

It was hard to believe that only ten minutes ago she'd been so happy, and now she was devastated. She told herself that this didn't have to mean the end of her scheme, that there had to be other nice single men in Serendipity Bay. She couldn't give up.

She was feeling too emotional to think straight. Maybe this was a good time to sit down and write more Charlotte stories. She'd done some terrific work the night before, when she was alone in the bedroom. Sierra put a curse on Charlotte so the girl's physical appearance would reflect her personality. It had been fun describing Charlotte as a horrific monster, really slimy and grotesque.

Then she realized she'd forgotten to bring her notebook that morning. She'd have to go back to the cottage and collect it. Maybe Charlotte would still be with her mother and Lily could work in the backyard.

But on the way back, it occurred to her that Charlotte might have brought her mother to the cottage, like Lily had advised her. What if Lily walked in on John and that woman making passionate love?

She was standing on the corner of the road, debating whether or not to go to the cottage, when she saw Charlotte coming her way. She was alone, which was a relief. Lily didn't want John and his ex-wife reuniting until she'd found someone for her mother.

She waited for Charlotte to reach her, figuring she might as well break the bad news about Martin. But as Charlotte got closer, Lily wondered if she had had some bad news of her own. Her eyes were red and puffy, and there were mascara streaks all around them.

Lily was taken aback. Charlotte Nettles...crying? Maybe it was an allergy.

"Did you get my text?" Lily asked her.

Charlotte didn't reply. And now, Lily definitely recognized the signs of her having been crying.

"What's wrong?"

"None of your business," Charlotte mumbled.

"Where's your mother?"

Now those tear-stained eyes were blazing. "Shut up, okay? Just shut up!"

She kept walking, in the direction of the cottage. Lily trotted along beside her. After a moment, she blurted out her own bad news.

"Martin's gay."

Charlotte shrugged. "Whatever."

"So he's not going to get together with my mother."

Charlotte just shrugged again.

"What about your mother and father?"

"It's not going to happen," Charlotte said through clenched teeth. "My mother's getting married to her boyfriend."

"Oh." After a moment, Lily ventured, "Want to talk about it?"

"Not with *you*," she snapped.

They entered the cottage. John was at the table, talking to an image on his PC screen, and his back was to them. The girls went into the bedroom.

Charlotte threw herself onto her bed and buried her face in the pillow. Lily just stood there, unsure of what to say or do. The room suddenly seemed oddly dark—or was that just her mood? No, she could hear the light tapping of a summer rain at the window. She wouldn't be going back to the beach.

"Guess I'll go take a shower," she said.

There was no response from the motionless body on the bed.

Lily spent more time than usual in the shower. She just stood there, letting the water fall down on her and imagining that it could wash away all her sadness. It didn't happen. When she finally emerged, she was feeling just as bad.

Her mother had returned—Lily could hear her and John talking in the kitchen. Lily went back into the bedroom.

Charlotte didn't have her head buried in a pillow anymore. She was sitting up, with an open notebook on her lap.

Lily's notebook.

"What are you doing with that?" Lily cried out.

Charlotte looked up. Her eyes were cold. "I'm reading it."

"How dare you? That's private!" Lily moved to snatch it away, but Charlotte held on to it tightly.

"How dare *you*? Calling me a monster!"

Lily was torn. She was furious that Charlotte had the nerve to open her notebook and read it. At the same, she wanted to defend herself.

"It's just a story—" she began, but Charlotte broke in.

"It's terrible! I can't believe how mean you are!"

Lily dropped any effort at defense. "How mean *I* am? You're the meanest person in the world! At least I only *write* about doing bad things. You actually *do* them!"

"Oh yeah? When was the last time I tried to smother you with a pillow?"

"How about all those times at school when you and your nasty friends made fun of me?" Lily shot back.

At least Charlotte didn't deny this. "You're such a geek, you deserve it."

Lily stared at her in disbelief. "You really think you're so superior?"

"You say it yourself, right in here." Charlotte tapped the notebook. "I'm somebody, and you're nobody."

"Oh, you're somebody, alright. Somebody evil and horrible and—and—" Desperately, she searched for the right word. "Repulsive! You're repulsive!"

"You're just jealous," Charlotte shot back.

"Are you crazy?" Lily shrieked. "I don't want to be like you or your awful friends!"

"Everyone wants to be like me and my friends," Charlotte yelled back.

"That's what you like to think, you and your evil pals."

"It's what we *know*!"

Lily was shaking with fury. "You disgust me!"

"You disgust me even more! I can't even bear to look at you. I hate you!" She threw the notebook at Lily.

Lily ducked to avoid it. And in doing so, she saw her mother and John standing in the doorway. Their eyes were wide, their mouths were open. But no words came out. They just stood there, looking totally stunned.

chapter seventeen

Something Charlotte had always admired about her father was the way he kept his cool. He was always calm, always in control. Even when Dahlia left him, he never lost it. She had never before seen him looking the way he looked now. Not angry, not upset, just completely shocked.

And Kate... she had a fair complexion, but now it was practically white.

Neither spoke. Nor did Charlotte. And Lily looked like she was frozen. The parents just stood there, they didn't come in. Then they stepped back, out of the room, and closed the door.

Lily picked her notebook up from the floor where it had landed and put it in her tote. Then she got on her bed, grabbed her book, and opened it.

Charlotte put in her earbuds. But she didn't turn on any

music—she just lay on her back and stared at the ceiling. After a couple of minutes, she realized Lily hadn't turned a page in her book. She wasn't really reading.

There was a light knock on the door, and then it opened. Her father stood there.

"Girls, could you come out here, please? We need to talk to you."

Lily put her book down and got up. Charlotte took off the headset. What now? she wondered. Another lecture about getting along? Would they be sent back to this room and ordered not to come out until they were friends? *That* wasn't going to happen.

Or maybe something worse. Her father and Kate would announce that they were going to get married, that she and Lily would be sisters, and they'd just have to deal with it.

They gathered around the dining table, the adults on one side, the girls on the other. Charlotte tried to read her father's expression. Not angry, but serious. And sad.

He looked at Kate. "Would you like to speak first?"

"It doesn't matter," Kate told him. "We're on the same page. But okay, I'll start." She turned to them.

"Lily, Charlotte...John and I have decided that this can't work. Despite the way he and I feel about each other, there isn't any way we can go on being together when you two are so unhappy. We see now that we'll never be able to bring you two together, and we can't be a family."

John spoke. "And if we can't be a family, there's no point in continuing our relationship. We've agreed about this."

Kate nodded. "Lily, we'll be taking the first train home tomorrow morning." She stood up and looked at the window. "I see it's stopped raining. I think I'll go for a walk."

Lily started to get up. "I'll come with you."

"No, Lily, I'd rather be alone." She left the table, picked up her bag, and walked out of the cottage.

John rose. "I've got some business calls to make." He left the room and went out into the backyard.

The cottage suddenly seemed terribly quiet. Charlotte broke the silence.

"Well. We got what we wanted."

Lily didn't respond.

"Aren't you happy?" Charlotte pressed. "*I* am."

Lily finally spoke. "Yeah, well, that's all that matters, right? You only think about yourself."

"Oh give me a break. You wanted this just as much as I did."

Lily rose and went into the bedroom. Charlotte remained at the table and wondered what she should do now, and why she didn't feel more relieved.

Maybe she was still depressed about Dahlia and Jay. Her mother was never coming back. At least now she wouldn't have to share her father.

He'd meet someone else, she felt sure of that. He was

handsome, he had plenty of money...there'd be other women in his life. None of whom came with Lily Holden. She didn't have to feel sorry for him.

But maybe he needed some comfort from his beloved one-and-only daughter. She'd tell him not to be sad, that there were other fish in the sea, something like that. She got up and went outside.

He wasn't on the phone. He was just sitting at the picnic table, staring at nothing. She stood behind him, put her arms around his neck, and kissed his cheek.

"Daddy..."

"What do you want, Charlotte?"

"Nothing! Just thought you might like to talk."

"I'm really not in the mood right now."

Actually, she didn't much feel like talking either.

"Okay. I guess I'll go to the beach."

He nodded absently.

Impulsively, she added, "Do you want to come?"

"No," he said.

She waited a moment, for one of his usual comments, like "Have fun" or "Be careful." But he said nothing. Almost like he didn't care what she did. Or maybe she just wasn't the person on his mind at that moment.

She didn't want to go back into the bedroom and see Lily, so she didn't change into her swimsuit or collect her tote. She just grabbed her phone from the table, stuck it in her pocket, and left.

Looking down at the beach from the top of the stairs, she saw that it was less crowded than usual. The rain had chased people away and they hadn't yet returned.

Behind her, she heard the roar of a motorcycle. Turning, she watched it pull up alongside her, and the driver took off his helmet.

"Hey, babe."

"Hi, Paul." It vaguely occurred to her that he was seeing her now without her usual makeup. She probably looked her age. He didn't seem to notice.

"I looked for you last night," he said. His tone was almost accusing.

"Oh. Yeah, well, something came up. Is that your brother's bike?"

"Cool, huh? Wanna go for a spin?"

She'd never been on a motorcycle in her life. Well, it would take her mind off things. She wouldn't keep seeing her father's sad face.

"Sure, why not?"

"Hop on."

As she climbed on behind him, he instructed her to put her arms around his waist.

And then they took off.

chapter eighteen

Lily loved to read, for many reasons. One of the main reasons was the fact that a good story could take you away from real life. And when you had problems, a book gave you a way to run away from them.

This book she'd been reading, *In Another World*, was particularly good for this, because it let you escape from the real world altogether.

But not this time. She found herself reading the same line over and over again. She kept trying to move on, because what else could she do? Her mother didn't want to be with her. She doubted very much that John would like her company either. She certainly didn't want to be anywhere near Charlotte. Just thinking about them all was bad enough.

She fell back on her bed, closed her eyes, and tried to

conjure up images of Darius, the handsome prince in Rulers of the Galaxy. What would happen to him in the next book? He was the youngest of the ruler's three sons, which meant he wasn't in line for the throne, and he was happy about that because he didn't want to be king.

But maybe some enemy would kill the eldest son. Then that would cause a battle, and the second son could be seriously injured. Darius would nurse him, but then the brother might die anyway, and everyone would think that Darius poisoned him or something because they wouldn't believe he doesn't want to be king. They'd take him to be hanged. But then the beautiful servant girl, Lily, would come to his rescue and they would run away together…

It was a very nice dream. But eventually she opened her eyes and realized she'd fallen asleep. She sat up and looked at the clock. Only two hours had passed. Now, what was she going to do?

She was thirsty. On her way to the kitchen, she passed the open door of the other bedroom. Her mother was in there, folding clothes and placing them in the open suitcase on her bed. She looked up and saw Lily.

"You need to pack your things," she said. "The train leaves at eight in the morning."

"Okay. Where's John?"

"He's jogging."

"Really? I haven't seen him do that since we got here."

"He only does it when he's feeling..." She didn't finish the sentence. She didn't have to.

"Mom..."

"Hm?"

"I'm sorry."

She waited for an automatic response, something like "That's okay, honey," or "I understand." Something like that, something that would make her feel better. But there was only silence.

It was broken by the sound of a phone ringing. Kate went into her bag and took out her phone.

"Hello?"

She looked puzzled. "Who? My daughter?" Then she gasped. "What happened? Yes, yes, of course! What's the name of the hospital again? Yes, I'll be right there!"

Lily stared at her mother in alarm. "What's going on?"

Her mother was hitting another button on her phone. "Charlotte's been in an accident."

From the dining room, another phone began to ring.

"Damn, John didn't take his phone!" Kate cried out. She hung up, and then hit something else on the phone screen.

"Hello, taxi?"

When she finished giving the address, she grabbed her bag.

"Do you know which way he went jogging?" Lily asked.

"No. When he comes home, tell him—"

Lily interrupted. "I want to go with you."

Kate didn't argue. She took a notepad, scribbled a note, and left the room to put it on the table. When she returned, she handed Lily her iPhone.

"Take your phone, my battery's almost dead."

Lily stuck it in her pocket, and they went outside to wait for the taxi. On the way to the hospital, they both watched the road for any sign of John, but they didn't see him.

"What happened?" Lily wanted to know. "Was she hit by a car? How bad is it?"

"I don't know," her mother said.

"Why did the hospital call you and not her father?"

"I don't know!" her mother exclaimed.

Lily couldn't remember ever having seen her mother so upset and worried. It didn't surprise her—Kate was a very caring person. What surprised her was that she was feeling kind of worried herself. Okay, maybe Charlotte was her least favorite person in the world, but she didn't wish her *dead*.

Then she recalled what she'd written in her notebook, the part where Sierra suffocates Charlotte with a pillow. Of course, wishful thinking didn't make something actually happen. But silently, she began to chant, *I didn't mean it, I didn't mean it.*

Inside the hospital, they followed the signs to the emergency room. Lily went with her mother to a desk, where a woman in a blue coat looked up.

"Yes? Can I help you?"

"I've come about Charlotte Nettles."

The woman went through some papers and frowned. "Who?"

Kate explained the phone call she'd received, and the woman extracted a sheet.

"Oh, that's her name." She wrote it down. "Your daughter was unconscious when she was brought in a half hour ago, and she didn't have any identification on her, just a cell phone. Fortunately, it wasn't locked. I found you in her contacts." She stood up. "This way, please."

She led them to a waiting area, where a few other anxious-looking people were seated. "Wait here, I'll get the doctor."

"But why did she call *you*, and not her father?" Lily wondered out loud again. "Or *her* mother?"

Kate didn't seem to have heard her. Lily pondered for a minute, and then it hit her. She fished the iPhone out of her pocket and turned it on.

The wallpaper on the screen was totally unfamiliar. It was Charlotte's phone. She must have picked up Lily's by mistake. It was locked, so she couldn't look at Charlotte's contacts. And the only name in Lily's contacts was "Mom."

A man in a white coat approached and called out, "Mrs. Nettles?"

Kate jumped up. "Yes, I'm . . . um, Mrs. Nettles. Where's Charlotte? How is she?"

"She's going to be fine," the doctor said. "She's regained

consciousness and there's no sign of a concussion or broken bones. We'd like to run a scan, just to make sure, if we have your permission. She suffered a deep cut on her forehead that required fifteen stitches."

"But what happened? Was she hit by a car?"

"No, she was riding on the back of a motorcycle. There was a sharp curve, and she was thrown from it." He shook his head in disapproval and added, "She wasn't wearing a helmet."

Kate turned to Lily in bewilderment. "What was Charlotte doing on a motorcycle?"

"I don't know!"

She turned back to the doctor. "Who was driving it?"

The doctor consulted his notes. "Someone named Paul, no last name. She said he's a boy she met on the beach."

Lily drew in her breath. "One of the hoodlums," she murmured.

"What?" Kate asked.

But Lily just gave another "I don't know" gesture. She wasn't going to be a snitch.

"What happened to the boy?" Kate asked the doctor.

The doctor did another disapproving headshake. "Nothing, it appears. He just took off."

Kate put a hand to her mouth.

Lily couldn't help herself. "He really *is* a hoodlum!"

Kate looked at her sharply. "Do you know who he is?"

Lily hesitated. Did she? He could be any one of the

three boys she'd seen with Charlotte. And for all she knew, Charlotte could still be madly in love with whoever he was. Although she *hoped* not, and Charlotte would have to be a total idiot if she still cared about him.

"No," she replied.

The doctor continued. "Fortunately, a passing motorist saw your daughter on the side of the road and called an ambulance."

"Can we see her?" Kate asked.

"Yes, of course." He let them down a hall to a curtained-off area.

In the white hospital gown, with no makeup, her hair pulled back, and a huge bandage covering her forehead, Charlotte looked like a child. A sad, hurt child.

To her own utter amazement, Lily burst into tears. Her mother rushed to the bedside and put her arms around Charlotte.

Now Charlotte was weeping. "I was so scared," she managed to say.

"I know, darling, I know," Kate crooned. "You poor child." Then *she* started crying too.

This was how John found them, all three of them on the bed, sobbing. Lily saw him first, standing in front of the curtain, sweaty, disheveled, still in his jogging shorts, his face ashen.

Then he was on the bed too. And crying with the rest of them.

chapter nineteen

Charlotte sat very still as she was wheeled away for her scan. By the time she returned, she was calm and all cried out. But very embarrassed to have cried in front of Lily Holden! What if she told people back at school?

On the other hand, she'd been in an accident, she'd had stitches, and she was lying in a hospital bed. She was entitled to cry. And to be perfectly honest, she didn't really think that Lily was mean enough to make fun of her in this condition. What she really didn't understand was that Lily had been crying too. But maybe she'd imagined that. She was feeling pretty woozy from the shot she'd been given for the pain.

The doctor returned and let everyone back into the room.

"You can take her home," he told them. "But keep an eye on her."

"Of course we will," Kate assured him.

He turned to Charlotte and his voice became stern. "And the next time you get on a motorcycle, wear a helmet!"

"There won't be a next time," her father said grimly. "Will there, Charlotte?"

She managed a weak smile. "No, Daddy."

The clothes she'd been wearing were brought in, but they looked pretty bad—torn and filthy. She looked at them in distaste.

"Do I have to put those on?"

"Just keep your hospital gown on," her father said. "I'll return it tomorrow."

She was glad to see that he was back to his usual totally-in-control behavior. But she wasn't thrilled about leaving the hospital in this white thing. What if she ran into someone she knew? Maybe she could ask them to go to the cottage and bring back something nicer for her to wear.

Lily seemed to know what she was thinking, and she drew closer. "It doesn't look that bad," she whispered. "And I'm sure my mother has her huge sunglasses in her bag. You can put them on and nobody will recognize you."

As John and Kate went out into the hall to fill out more paperwork, a man came in with a wheelchair.

"I can walk," Charlotte said as she started to get out of the bed.

"Hospital policy," he answered.

When her feet hit the floor, she realized she *was* a little unsteady. The man took one arm and Lily took the other to help her into the chair.

They left the hospital and followed the parents into the parking lot where her father had left the car.

"I'm glad you're okay," Lily said.

Charlotte was about to utter an automatic "thank you" and then remembered who she was talking to. She turned her head to the side and looked up at her.

"Like you care."

Lily shrugged. "I sort of do. At least I'm glad you're not dead."

For once, Charlotte had to agree with her. "Yeah, me too. But I'm worried about this cut on my head."

"It's going to heal."

"Yeah, but it will leave a scar."

"It'll probably fade."

"Maybe. But what am I going to do till it does? I don't think makeup will cover it."

"You could get bangs cut," Lily suggested. "That would hide a scar."

Charlotte considered this. It wasn't a bad idea. And bangs were in style again, she'd seen pictures in *Teen Vogue*. Her friend Ashley had talked about getting bangs cut this summer.

"Yeah, I could do that. I think I'll go to the salon on

Main Street tomorrow." After a minute, she said, "You know, you should come with me."

"Why?" Lily asked.

"Because you need a haircut. You'd look a lot better with shorter hair. And nobody our age wears a braid."

"*I* do," Lily retorted. "And I'm *somebody*." Then she added, "Besides, we're leaving tomorrow, remember?"

The earlier events of the day came back to her, and Charlotte turned away. Looking straight ahead, she watched her father and Kate walking in front of them.

They were holding hands.

She nudged Lily, and pointed.

"Maybe not."

END